Shadowangel

Tim Capehart

Shadowangel

Tim Capehart

Shadowangel

Copyright © 2013 Timothy Capehart

Book design and cover illustration by Timothy Capehart
First Edition
Library of Congress Cataloging-in-Publication Data
Capehart, Tim
    Shadowangel / by Tim Capehart.
    168 p. ; 20 cm.
    Summary: Sixth-grader Josh moves with his mother to the town where she grew up and along with his new friend Marylis discovers a monster preying on the townspeople.
    ISBN-13: 978-1484920169
    ISBN-10: 1484920163
    [PZ7.C3744 2013]
    [FIC]—dcc22 CIP

This one is dedicated to
my nieces and nephews
Hausfelds, Hewitts and Stephensons
And all the kids who've called me
Mr. Tim

PROLOGUE

The eyes were the only bit of his hobby that Mr. Mikaplike found slightly...disturbing. Popping out the milky, jelly-filled, sometimes leaky eyes could be a problem for people who were weak of stomach. That part didn't bother him a bit. He could pop 'em out and toss 'em out without blinking one of his own eyes. For Mr. Mikaplike, the bead glass eyes that had to be slipped into the empty eye sockets once he'd finished all his other work on a carcass, THEY bothered him; more than that, they gave him the shivering jim-jams.

When he'd started stuffing animals for fun in the 1950's, Mr. Mikaplike had kept his supply of unused glass eyes in one of his mother's empty Mason jars. All those realistic, disembodied little eyes staring out at him day after day had started to fray his teenage nerves. Anyone who has done any taxidermy knows that working on the delicate bits of a project with shaking hands could make for a lumpy schnauzer or weasel or fox, so he had decided long ago to

1

keep the replacement glass eyes sorted by color and size in carefully labeled, totally opaque boxes.

He flipped over the yellow-orange cat that lay on his workbench; its empty eye sockets glared up at him. He'd avoided doing the eyeball-bit for weeks, but now Mrs. Tanner had called complaining about his taking so long. She'd said she needed her Jasper back as soon as possible.

As he reached for the box labeled "yellow-green/ cat/small," something landed on the roof of his workshop with an echoey, hollow thud.

Dang kids, Mr. Mikaplike thought. *I'd best go let them know I'm on to them and their scaliwagging tricks.* He worked at night for the express reason that the neighbor kids, at least the youngest of them, would be in bed and therefore quiet. That, and at 85, he didn't need all that much sleep. Taxidermy kept him occupied. He didn't hold stock with modern technologies. TV drained your brain and that Internet was ten times worse. He hated sleeping, always had. Who wanted to spend six, seven, eight hours dead-to-the-world especially when you were going to be...well, dead-to-the-world for good before too long?

He shuffled past some of his completed projects: beaver, poodle, parrot, owl. Each of them posed and looking, if he did say so himself, natural. He opened the side door of his garage workshop. The night air felt too dang cool for September. He stepped out and was surprised to find that the house next door was as dark as his. The two Beaumont brothers, who caused more trouble than any ten boys should, were nowhere in sight. If they were out and about and instigating problems, likely there'd be a light on somewhere in their house. Mr. Mikaplike didn't detect so much as a nightlight, and there was nothing wrong with his 20-20's. The blue-white pools of light from the streetlamp and the security light on the side of his house were empty. There was no ball anywhere he could see and no kids giggling, no whispering in the shrubbery. Mr. Mikaplike shrugged and grumbled without saying anything even he could put into actual words.

He turned to go in, but paused with the door half shut behind him. Despite the lack of Beaumont-bedevilment, something still felt wrong. The normally talkative katydids and crickets were silent. Even the frogs that lived in Sand Street Pond and the night birds that never seemed to shut up were quiet.

Odd.

Looking back on eighty-some years there was quite a bit "odd" he'd put an eye to. He shrugged again and closed the door.

Walking back to his workbench, he rubbed the large black mole on his cheek, as he often did when he was lost in thought. Unfamiliar territory, his father would have said. Mr. Mikaplike snorted a chuffing approximation of a laugh. Maybe it was a live cat scaring all the night creatures into silence. Mrs. Tanner herself had a good five more felines, and she lived just up the street. The dense woods surrounding the town harbored any number of critters that could have ventured into the neighborhood to cause a silence.

He reached for Jasper.

Something in the shadowy dark by the freezer beneath the window scraped the concrete floor.

Mr. Mikaplike squinted into the blackness.

Another scrape like a chain or a claw. This one followed by a wet, squelchy thud like a bag of wet sand landing on the ground.

"W-who's there?" he stepped back toward the side door. His hands, still outstretched to pick up the dead cat, rose slightly in anticipation of an attack and his knobbly knuckles curled into loose fists.

Silence. The uncanny quiet outside seemed to leech the sounds from the workshop. His old heart set to racing.

Mr. Mikaplike reached for one of his hide knives on the pegboard wall next to the door…

Something large and black shot out of the shadows at him. He felt claws grip first one arm and then the other. A thing darker than his shadowy workshop touched his flat, bulby nose. Mr. Mikaplike opened his mouth to scream at the pain of the claws digging in to his biceps, at the amorphous blackness that covered his face like a inky, amoeboid squid…but quite suddenly there was light, bright light filling his eyes and a calmness like he'd never felt.

Everything fell away.

Mr. Mikaplike slumped to the floor. His sightless gaze added one more glassy stare to his line of projects.

For a moment, his shallow breathing was accompanied, by alternating scrapes and squelchy thuds. After a few seconds of silence, there was a loud snap followed by fluttering rush and the sound of wings. Then the silence returned.

1

"I never asked to move to this weird, little town!" Josh yelled at his mother...or at least he did in his imagination. Josh would never really yell at his mother.

He hadn't yelled at her when she told him they were divorcing his father. He hadn't yelled at her when she told him he had to leave his friends and his school behind so they could move. He hadn't even yelled at her when she told him they were moving to Rock Hollow (which was about as close to nowhere as you could get without catching a flight to Antarctica). Complain loudly? Well...maybe. Yell? No.

They'd left Dayton to move to Rock Hollow because she'd gotten a job teaching fifth grade at her old elementary school, Benjamin Harrison Elementary. Only Rock Hollow would name a school after a president the history books described as "largely forgotten" and "politically inept." Sure the guy was born in Ohio, but nowhere near Rock Hollow; and as US Presidents go he was a pretty big loser. Just because you got elected President didn't mean you couldn't be a looser. Though in the guy's defense, he had some stiff competition; who could live up to Abraham Lincoln and Franklin Roosevelt?

Josh's Mom had moved them into a creepy, little house close—too close if you asked Josh—to his Granma Reece who was…well you might say…being nice you'd call her…Oh heck, she was nutty as a jar of Planters.

Granma Reece was part of the reason he hated Rock Hollow. Josh certainly did not hate his grandmother. She could be fun—in small doses—like it used to be: short visits on the big holidays and an occasional family holiday. However, spending all or part of everyday with her was, to use one of his mother's favorite words, "trying."

Granma Reece had 500 stories about every relative in every generation of all branches of their family tree. If half of the stories were even half-true, the family could have made a fortune by opening its own freak show a couple of generations back. All those tales were bad enough, but she didn't stop there. Granma was the retired Rock Hollow Town Librarian, so she had a ton of stories about everyone else in town (and all the treenuts on every branch of their family trees back to the days of the pilgrims). And Granma's repertoire made Rock Hollow sound like the hot bed of super-weird in America. The Addams Family would

7

fit right in...no, they'd be the boringly normal family everyone talked about.

Now that school had started, every day after his sixth grade class let out, Josh had a choice: he could wait around the school where the only safe place for a teacher's kid was in her classroom, or he could walk to Granma Reece's creepy, big house and wait for his mother. If—and this had only happened a couple of times so far—he was really unlucky, Granma would be substituting for the new Town Librarian Miss Picturtle at the public library, and Josh would have to go there. Granma would invariably put him to work. She would either have him inching up and down the aisles of dust-caked books making sure each book was in the right place on the shelves, or she would have him clean the newly returned books. The former could make you go blind after an hour or so of staring at all of those tiny numbers and letters. That was preferable to the latter which made Josh queasy. You never knew just what that sticky, brown, crusty stuff on the cover or between the pages might once have been. Coulda been a bug; coulda been a booger...coulda been something far worse than either. Note to library book readers: ginormous cock-roaches, no matter how dry and flat, should never be used as bookmarks. Also bacon, raw or cooked is a poor choice of place holder.

Today he was "lucky." He was heading to Granma's house as he was imagining yelling at his mother. Imagining her seeing his very well made points about his needing to be with his friends and about how Rock Hollow's weird would warp him and its dull would kill his brain. Imagining her seeing his points and packing everything up. Imagining them moving right back to Dayton and into their old house with his dad.

"Yeah, right," Josh said sarcastically, swinging his book bag at nothing. The weight of it, pulling him further along the sidewalk, felt good. He swung it again. And again. And again letting it tug him forward each step because he certainly did not want to take those steps on his own.

Granma's whopper stories aside, Rock Hollow wasn't gross or anything. There were no big factories barfing out black smoke or rundown buildings or gangs or crime. Everyone worked in the twist tie factory in the hollow to the east or the joke and novelty factory in the hollow to the west. Josh had only recently learned that a "hollow," or "holler" as it sounded when some people said it, was what they called a valley between ridges in south-central Ohio. He'd always thought it was just a part of the town's name. Josh knew that some adults even lived in Rock Hollow and commuted to Cincinnati. He pegged them as prime candidates for the loony bin. Only a crazy person would voluntarily live in Rock Hollow and drive through all those nice, normal suburbs to work in the city and return here each night.

As he walked, he breathed deeply. The September breeze brought the hint of winter scent of pines from the surrounding woods. The leafy trees made tunnels of the streets and kept things cool despite the heat which you only felt if you stayed in the sun for too long. If there were just more stores, more theaters, more...anything, Rock Hollow really wouldn't be so bad. Though, it would still be hours from his friends, and that was bad enough.

He stopped walking.

He shuddered.

He had arrived.

There was nothing remotely house-like about Granma Reece's house. It looked as if it had escaped from a cemetery. It was all gray stone. Not, you must understand, bricks of gray stone held together by mortar; that would be too normal. Each wall was one great slab of gray rock. It looked as if it had been chiseled out of some extraordinarily square, unbelievably huge native boulder. There were steps leading down to the small front porch and filigree-topped half-pillars on either side of the door. (What exactly was the purpose of a fake half-pillar cut into the wall? Pillars should hold something up, right? That was kind of the definition of a pillar). Whatever wasn't gray stone was black wrought iron. The whole thing was too short, too fat, too big, and too gray.

"Howdie Josh-B'gosh!"

Josh bit his tongue hard to keep his promise to his mother not to curse. He hated that nickname. J, Josh, Joshie, Joshua Anthony Cotter anything was better than that nickname. It was something you'd call a preschooler not a sixth grader. Granma was the only one who still used it. He looked around the front yard, but didn't see her. It had actually sounded as if—

Josh shaded his eyes with one hand and looked up.

Granma was waving from the flat part of the roof high above the front door. She had a pair of binoculars in the hand that wasn't performing the continuous, apoplectic wave.

Josh just stared and performed a mental face-palm.

With her poofy, white hair teased into a bulging mound on top of her head and the sun behind her casting her eyes into shadow, Granma looked more than a little like one of those gray aliens from Close Encounters. *Appropriate*, Josh thought with a smirk. *She's an alien all right!*

"Come on up," she said. "The window's open in your Uncle Cecil's old room. I popped out the screen."

"What are you doing?" Josh yelled.

"I'm watching the Nicholsons next street over." She stopped waving to point.

"What?" He said. He wasn't sure he'd heard her correctly. Was she spying on the neighbors in broad daylight perfectly visible on top of the house? Josh looked in the direction she'd pointed. He couldn't see over the house across the street, which wasn't the Nicholson's. He did, however, hear very faint, strange, rousing music.

"They're powerful fond of Opera," Granma said putting the binoculars up to her eyes. "Every day about this time when Mr. Nicholson gets home from the plant, the whole family gets together and acts out a scene or two from an opera." She looked back down at Josh. "They're half way through Wagner's 'Ring Cycle.' They've been working on it for months. Come on up. Their outfits are a hoot!"

Josh shook his head. She was probably making it all up or seeing things. He listened. The music could be opera. In Dayton as a member of the Muse Machine Fine Arts Club, Josh had been to a couple operas at the Victoria Theater downtown. He knew people who were fans of opera, but no one dressed up in silly Viking costumes and pranced around their living rooms lip-syncing to Wagner. They just didn't, not even in Rock Hollow.

"No thanks," he said probably not even loud enough for her to hear. "I'll be in the kitchen when you're done."

She said something more, but he was already inside with the big, gray, wooden door shut firmly behind him.

2

The inside of the house was stranger, if that was possible, than the outside. Josh was sure it had been built as some sort of tourist attraction or maybe the architect designed it on a dare. There were staircases, like the one in the entrance hall, which went nowhere and ended in a blank wall. There were rooms on the first floor you could only get into through windows from the outside. And there were doors that opened on to nothing but brick all over the house. He'd grown up visiting it, so he sort of knew his way around. He walked past a dead-end hallway they used for storage and past a doorframe that framed a blank piece of wall rather than a door and then climbed into the kitchen through an open "window" set in the left-hand side of the front corridor's back hall.

Granma didn't come down from the roof as Josh had kind of expected her to. He foraged through her cabinets looking for a snack. Of course, her idea of a snack was a big, old wad of celery without even any peanut butter on it. He wasn't about to open the vegetable crisper to look for a snack. That is where the foods you were forced to eat dwelt. The best he could come up with was a Tupperware bin of what looked like oatmeal raison cookies that he found in the back of one of her cupboards behind the brewer's yeast and quinoa whatever the heck those were. The cookies were a little too chewy and kind of salty really, but he was on his second when his mother arrived through the back door rather than through the window from the hall.

"How was your day, J?" She asked as she walked into the kitchen.

"Same," he said looking at her but only as far as the briefcase in her hand. "Terrible, as always. Can we move home please?"

She sat down heavily with a sigh that sounded as if it had clawed its way up from her toes. "Josh, please give it a chance," she said with a tired back-of-the-throat crackle in her voice that made Josh want to give her a glass of water and nearly made him sorry for bugging her. "We've only been here a month—"

"One month, three days, two hours." He made a show of looking at his wrist which was not sporting a watch at present. "And twenty-four minutes."

She gave him a look that would have said "cool it, buster" if she didn't already appear on the verge of falling asleep. Her eyes were only about half open, and her hair seemed to be making a wild attempt to frizz its way out of her ponytail. "This is home now, J," she said with a little shake of her head.

"It doesn't have to be home. We could move back to Dayton." Josh knew they'd been over this a bunch of times, but he also knew that with parents repetition sometimes paid off.

"J, this is where we live. This is where my job is."

"There are schools in Dayton, Mom. They would hire you. This place is truly, utterly bizarre."

"I grew up here, and I didn't turn out so bad."

Grudgingly, he smiled at her. "No, but it couldn't have been this weird when you were a kid."

She looked at him for a moment blinking slowly. Then with a two-armed gesture that encompassed the entire room, she said, "Josh, look at this house. Rock Hollow has always been a little—different." She took the elastic band from around what was left of her ponytail, shook out her hair, and refastened it in a neater tail.

"A little?" He said thinking of what the Nicholsons may or may not be doing one block over. "If I promise to give it a chance, can I just go back to our house after school? I'm eleven almost twelve. Why do I need to come here or go to the library?" He picked up another cookie.

"We'll talk about it, J. I'd really rather not leave you alone. We eat with Mom sometimes, and—"

"Why don't we just move in then? That way Granma can baby-sit me whenever you're not around."

"J," she said with another, shallower sigh. "You know why—"

Granma stuck her head in through the window frame before his mother could finish; and one hand to her chest, the other extended into the room toward the ceiling she shrieked, "Yo ho ho-oooh! Yo ho ho-oooh!" She waggled her head left and right smiling insanely and looking as if she'd just bitten something in half. "Just watchin' them makes me want to take to the stage myself. I've got an opera singer's voice!"

"Better give it back," said Josh's mom with a sly smile.

"That one's two days older than dirt, Lisa," Granma said as she climbed through the window. The binoculars that hung around her neck bounced off her T-shirt, which read, "Beam me up, Scotty. This planet sucks." She opened her mouth to say something else but stopped. After looking at Josh for a moment with an expression between shock

17

and concern, she said, "Like those barley and date cookies, Josh-B'gosh?"

Josh gaped with horror at what would have been his third cookie. He set it back in the bin and raked his teeth across his tongue in an attempt to scrape away all traces of those cookies he'd finished.

"It's my own special recipe," Granma said. "I'll make you a batch. I don't like 'em myself, but your Grandad doted on 'em."

Josh felt the first two cookies creeping up his throat, and he swallowed hard to send them back down. His Grandad had been dead for over five years. Surely those cookies hadn't...Josh shuddered for the second time in an hour.

"Staying for diner, Lisa?" Granma asked.

"I don't think so, Mom. We'll stay tomorrow though."

"Rightee-oo!" Granma said. She kissed each of them on the top of their head and left the way she'd come.

After a moment of silence, his mom asked "What was that opera stuff about?"

"I don't believe it myself. Can we just pretend it didn't happen?"

His mother smiled. "Come on J, let's blow this popsicle stand."

He let her hug him, and he sort of hugged her back.

She held him at arm's length and said, "Walk me to my car? I left it at the school."

"Why would you do that?" He asked as they headed for the back door.

"You really want to know? You'll think I'm a goon."

"Too late."

She punched him lightly on the shoulder. "When I stepped out of the school, I kind of felt like I was back *in* school. I just wanted to walk home for old time's sake."

"Are you sure you didn't just forget you drove to work today?" he said with a sly smile of his own.

She punched him again propelling him up the back stairs toward what was actually ground level in the side yard. He held the mulberry bush that hid the opening of the stairwell aside and let his mother exit first. Josh smiled at her and followed her along the outside wall of the house to the street. Now he really felt like a heel for needling her to move home. She was home. He knew he would let her hold his hand on the way back to Benjamin Harrison because it would make her happy. He just hoped none of the kids from school would see them. They already avoided talking to him. He didn't want them laughing at him and calling him "Momma's Boy" as well. Life in Rock Hollow was already horrifying enough.

3

The next afternoon in school Josh looked at the clock for what had to be the ten millionth time. He would swear on any stack of books, holy or unholy, that negative two minutes had passed since the last time he looked. The clock's hands were definitely moving backward.

Once again this period Josh had shaken himself awake just in time to save himself from knocking his forehead against his desk. Science class, his last period of the day, always dragged. Mr. Stacey, the teacher, seemed to have a strange effect on time. He could make 50 minutes seem like 15 hours. He was, at that moment, droning on about igneous rocks. His low voice sounded like the constant hum of an old, electric alarm clock buzzing toward its last days. The weirdest thing was that his voice was only low when he lectured like it was a put-on voice-of-authority or something. The rest of the time he sounded—and looked for that matter—like that Squidward from the SpongeBob cartoon only without so many legs.

One good thing about Benjamin Harrison Elementary was that sixth graders had their day broken into six periods "to prepare them for the rigors of junior high school while still in the familiar setting of grammar school." Or so read the new student orientation booklet they'd made him read his first day. Well, it did make the day go faster...until you hit Science class. And if you really hated one teacher, at least there would be a different one in less than an hour. Josh had finished reading the whole science book a week ago. It was so old, he was sure someone in one of the classes had a copy with his mom's name written in the front. In the text Pluto was still a planet. The Brontosaurus was still a real dinosaur. And computers were still huge boxy white things with single color screens. It was also really easy stuff. So he was stuck in Strangeville USA, and he was destined to be bored to boot. Science had been one of his favorite subjects in Dayton.

Last night, at least, he'd gotten his mother to agree to let him walk home instead of to Granma Reece's or the library from now on...except on days when they were going to have dinner at her house—like tonight.

His mother was a worrier, but she wasn't mean or unreasonable...usually. To win his point, he'd just reminded her that he was: 1) eleven, 2) responsible, and 3) now living in a town where the worst crime of this century and the last had involved the chance meeting of some overdue library books and a hungry goat. She'd seen reason.

The bell rang.

Josh looked at the ceiling and gave thanks to whoever might be listening that for 23 hours, at least, Science class was over...he followed that with a silent but insistent wish that Granma would not serve liver for dinner tonight, which she did all too often.

"Before you go, class," now that he wasn't lecturing, the pitch of Mr. Stacey's voice wavered so much it sounded like he had a slide-whistle stuck in his throat. "Don't forget to read chapter two tonight. You'll like it," he smiled. "Evolution is grrr-oovy!"

Josh stopped gathering his books and stared at his teacher through slitted eyes.

Mr. Stacey was making the "thumbs up" sign with both hands. His expression made him look as if he'd just been punched in the face. He smiled and wiggled his thumbs in jerky circles while nodding vigorously at each student as they filed out of the classroom.

Josh was dumfounded at the sheer geeky horror of the man. He wanted to drop everything and run. Run out of the classroom. Run out of the school. Run right out of Rock

Hollow. Run until he was back where people were at least in the neighborhood of sanity.

Instead he picked up the last of his books, smiled what felt like a sickly smile at Mr. Stacey, and followed the rest of the students out into the hall.

His mom's classroom was only one floor up. Josh had been thinking about waiting for her, but now he just wanted out. He shoved everything he didn't need into his locker, which, since school was too easy for words, was everything he was carrying except for his book bag and the books he was reading for fun, and hurried down the stairs.

He made it as far as the bottom of the front steps of the school building, before something large and hard landed on his shoulder and forced him to spin around.

That something was a hand and it was attached to the rest of Hannibal Liss.

Before he moved to Rock Hollow, Josh had thought that the "school bully" thing had gone out with the Eighties; it was old fashioned to think that there was one big, mean (usually dumb) kid who was feared the whole school over. These days when you said "bully" in the real world, everyone thought "anonymous kids on the Internet." Sure there were still mean kids in every district that occasionally did nasty things to the small and the young…but no one kid the whole school (including some teachers) trembled at the thought of; that just seemed so "Growing Pains"…Rock Hollow proved itself behind the times here too. Hannibal had been held back twice and was mad at everyone and everything. Besides that, he was what polite people called "big-boned" and what kids with a death wish called "fatty-fatty bom-bi-latty." One of the two kids who had talked to Josh in the past three weeks of school had warned him that Han Liss makes sure all the new kids know who rules the school.

Guess it's that time, Josh thought as he faced the tower of bully.

Han smiled. Which only served to make him look even more like a giant, demented Cabbage Patch Kid doll. "Hey Josh Cracker," he said.

Ha, Cracker-Cotter how witty! Josh thought. Before he could stop himself, he replied, "You grew up in *this* town and you're calling *me* Cracker?"

Hannibal's tiny, close-set eyes squinted.

He's thinking, Josh thought. *If he's as slow as I've heard, I might get away before he puts it together that I just insulted him.* Josh turned to run and ran smack into one of Hannibal's Goons.

The Goon grabbed for Josh.

Josh ducked. He stomped on a foot (since it wasn't his own, it must have belonged to one Goon or another). Ducked a second Goon. Kicked a shin, and ran.

It wasn't until he heard Hannibal yell from a distance, "You won't get away next time, Cracker," that Josh dared to look around while still running. Hannibal and his Goons hadn't even bothered to give chase. One Goon was laughing; the other was bouncing on one foot and rubbing the other foot. Hannibal was shaking a fist in Josh's direction. His long arms and chunky body made him look like a genetic experiment gone horribly wrong, a Cabbage Patch Gorilla Baby.

Josh did not stop running until Granma's house got in his way.

4

For dinner that night: liver, of course. And two voices saying, "Try it. You've never had it fixed this way." And, in this instance, there was truth in that cliché of motherspeak. Josh had never had liver wrapped in bacon, battered, and deep-fried in pork fat. He sat through the whole meal wondering how Granma, the Celery-Snacking Queen, could make such an artery-hardening cholesterol feast.

No matter how it is fixed, liver is liver is liver, Josh thought as he sat on the curb in front of Granma's house. No matter how you doctor it up, liver still stinks, and it tastes worse than it smells! He was sucking on a mint trying to get rid of the deep-fried-scab taste that had taken up residence in his mouth and hoping it would take away his liver breath too. Not that he could foresee talking to anyone in the near future who might get a whiff, but he didn't want to offend himself. For Christmas, he had already decided that he was getting his Granma a puppy. He'd tell her it was a gift so she wouldn't be lonely since he wasn't coming to her house every day after school. It would really be a convenient gross food dispose-all for him. He would train it to sit under his chair at every meal, and he'd discretely slip it everything inedible from his plate…he'd have to find a breed with a strong stomach and a weak sense of smell.

He'd told them he was going for a little walk…might as well walk. Maybe the motion of his legs would pull some idea from his head, an idea of a way, any way, to make things better.

He walked down Sand Street talking out loud to himself, "Mom is obviously happy here, and Dad's too busy for me in Dayton." He still wasn't sure how he felt about the whole divorce thing. He certainly wasn't happy with the way things had turned out. His parents had made their decision; they didn't want to live with each other anymore. Did it matter at all to anyone that Josh still wanted to live with both of them? "Survey says: nope!" Josh kicked a rock into the street and watched it skitter into the sewer grate at the opposite curb.

He turned the corner, kicking everything that looked the slightest bit kickable in his path. "There isn't one person I've met here who's normal enough to even think about trying to be friends." He gestured toward the sky with both hands. "And now I'm talking to myself! I'll fit right in before you know it."

He'd left a whole group of friends at home in Dayton. So what if they were only three hours away by car. It's not as if any of them could drive. Three hours away might as well be three hundred. By the time they are old enough to drive, they won't be friends anymore. Sure, Mom could tell him to write them, call them, e-mail them, even video-chat, but that was no way to sustain a friendship. None of his friends would write back, call back, e-mail back…and chat had, even in three short weeks, become a depressing list of all the things THEY were doing together. They all had each other to distract themselves. If they hadn't already forgotten about him, they didn't need him. Josh needed to talk, write, whatever; and he didn't have anyone.

It was getting darker, but the streetlights hadn't come on yet. There was still enough light to make the trees cast shadows. It was sort of half night. The sun was still up, but it had passed behind the ridge that encircled the hollow. No one was on the street. *What do these people do?* Josh wondered. Any other town and there would be kids out playing or goofing off. People should be out doing yard work or exercising or walking dogs or something. *This empty stillness is just plain creepy,* Josh thought, and he shivered.

It never got this cold in September in Dayton. He turned another corner. "And now I have this Han Liss freak on my back!" Josh said loudly shoving his hands in his pockets. "I shoulda just let him beat me up," he went on mumbling to himself. "Then maybe he would just leave me alone."

"Nope, doesn't work," came a voice from out of the night.

Josh jumped. He looked around. He couldn't see anyone anywhere around him. He was in one of those tree-branch tunnels between houses. The street outside of the tree tunnel looked pretty darn light in comparison...and pretty far away. Josh reminded himself that he was in safe little, strange little Rock Hollow; but he still felt a prickle of fear scurry up from the base of his spine like a spider with pin feet. He thought about pretending he hadn't heard anything, but pretending you didn't hear something is the same as admitting you did hear something. He looked around again. All he could see was a clump of bushes getting more and more shadowy in the dusk. "What? Who's there?" His voice was wavery and his heart was pounding a conga rhythm in his chest.

A head popped out of the bushes. It was a girl about eight or nine years old wearing thick glasses. All Josh could see of her were the shiny lenses of her glasses and her widely grinning mouth. *A Cheshire Cat with bad vision*, he thought.

"I said," the girl continued. "That even if you let Han beat you half-silly, it doesn't mean he'll leave you alone in the future. If he notices a person, he usually hits them. It's how he communicates."

"And you know all about him?" Josh put his hands on his hips, relief swelling his confidence.

"I should, his bedroom is right down the hall from mine," she stepped out of the bushes.

"I'm sorry," Josh said. "I mean . . .not that I'm sorry you're his sister—"

"Why not?" she said exaggerating the question by leaning toward him and raising both her hands above her head. "I'm sorry I'm his sister; he's a total butt."

Josh laughed in spite of himself and caught himself thinking she was kind of cute. She certainly didn't look anything like her brother. She was short and thin. The glasses were a bit on the thick side, but they weren't so thick that her eyes looked like oysters or anything. Her hair was neat and pulled back in a ponytail. There was some feathery thing sitting on her head where her ponytail was tied. Josh said, "That's a weird looking ponytail-holder."

The ponytail-holder hopped up and turned its head to stare at him with one tiny, black, glassy eye. Josh jumped back, his arms pin-wheeling for balance. He let out a startled cry.

"Jeez, It's just a parakeet," the girl said. "What are you from Mars or something?"

Josh felt foolish, but it had startled him. "It just surprised me," he said. "Aren't you afraid it'll...well, you-know, in your hair."

"Max isn't stupid," she said. "He knows to take a hike—or, I guess, a flight when he has to do that." She stepped forward and thrust out her hand. "Marylis Liss," she said. "And please don't make any jokes about stuttering."

Josh shook her hand. "Josh Cotter."

"That's what I thought," she said. "You're new, and we don't get a lot of new around here. Your mom's my teacher," she smiled. "She's great."

Josh smiled too. "Thanks." So Marylis was in fifth grade. She was either older than she looked or she had been moved ahead in school. Of course, at Benjamin Harrison intelligent spider monkeys would be likely candidates for skipping grades...Josh noticed an uncomfortable silence brewing. "Uh...so what were you doing in the bushes?"

"Lookin' for a frog," she said with half of a shrug. "Han usually just annoys me. Today when he got home from school, he was completely unbearable. He actually hit me, so he's got to pay."

Josh was completely confused. "Huh?" he said.

"He's terrified of frogs," she said with a hint of anger in her voice and a smartly evil gleam in her eye.

"What is scary about a frog? That is so weird," Josh said. He opened his mouth to apologize for calling her brother weird but stopped. Even though he'd only known her for a couple minutes, he had a strong feeling that Marylis would agree with him. "What exactly are you going to do with this frog?"

She mimed deep thought for a moment, pursing her lips, squinting at the sky, and tapping one finger on her cheek. "Well, usually I just shake it in front of his face and watch his piggy, little eyes quiver in fright. This time...this time I think it goes in his bed...maybe in his pillowcase."

They both laughed loudly, startling a few birds from the trees above their heads.

"Want some help?" Josh asked raising his eyebrows.

She half-smiled and nodded as she slid back into the shrubs.

Josh crawled into the bushes after her.

5

On the other side of the bushes, they bent double beneath low branches and followed a yellow, dirt path to the tiny pond that lay between Granite and Sand Streets. The trees and bushes opened a little over the pond, and the reflection of the pale-gray sky of evening made the water almost white. The two of them crept around the pond. The air was cooler close to the water. It felt almost wet around Josh's ankles. Dragonflies stirred the mist that sat just above the water's surface in lazy, dancing spirals looking, from a distance, quite a bit like Josh's idea of fairies. He heard a frog croak. He pointed, but Marylis was already headed in the right direction.

Without warning, orchestral music blared from somewhere nearby.

"Oh, Jeez," Marylis said without interrupting her froggy pursuit.

Josh looked at the back of her head, which meant he was staring at Max. The parakeet's bluish plumage looked violet in the evening dimness. Max was looking back at Josh with one curious eye. Josh scrunched up his nose and stuck out his tongue at the bird. To Marylis he said, "Please don't say that's the Nicholsons acting out an opera. My Grandmother said they did that, but—" his sentence remained half-finished because Marylis had turned around, and she was nodding.

Violins screeched. Something with a reed tweeted. And a voice that could put bats out of commission hit a high note.

Josh giggled. "Let's go look."

They sneaked through the bushes following the music toward the Nicholson's house and stood on tiptoe to peer in a living room window.

A chunky woman in a horned hat with long, yarn braids was beating at her armored chest. On the other side of the room, two girls dressed in long white gowns were "singing" something. Josh couldn't understand the words, but that was part of what made opera, opera; if they were singing in English, it would just be a super-melodramatic musical. The movement of their lips was synchronized with the singers' voices. *Do they actually sing under the music?* Josh wondered. Or, and this was just too sick and wrong to consider for long, did they practice before performing? What he really wondered was why anyone would do anything so—bizarre. A big man strode into the room toting a spear and seeming to shout at the ceiling. Josh noticed one of Han's Goons was apparently a Nicholson. The guy looked a wee bit different from (and a lot less intimidating than) the last time Josh had seen him. Now, Goon #1 had on a cock-eyed, horned hat and a bumpy breastplate that glistened in the lamplight. The armor was about four sizes too big for his skinny teenage chest. That was funny enough, but he was also wearing a leather skirt. Josh was pleased to see that when Goon #1 walked he favored his left foot. *The results of a recent, well-deserved stomp on the right foot*, Josh thought.

He covered his mouth and pointed.

Marylis covered her mouth too.

Both of them were laughing so much and trying so hard not to be heard or seen by anyone inside that they almost missed a sound that was out of place in the otherwise quiet evening air.

There was a dull thud high above their heads as if someone had thrown a basketball against the second-story wall or maybe dropped one on the roof. They stopped laughing and looked at each other.

Both shrugged.

They stepped away from the house being careful to stay out of the line of sight of anyone within who might happen to glance out. Both Josh and Marylis looked up.

Once they were far enough from the window, Josh asked as quietly as he could, "Their music's pretty loud...do you think they vibrated a window loose?"

Marylis shrugged again.

They both kept backing up and looking up at the house.

Josh saw the thing first.

Without knowing why, he suddenly felt very afraid. For the second time in one night he was aware that his heart rate quickened. He could feel his pulse in his neck and behind his eyes.

Something approximately kid-sized and very black lay on the little piece of roof just beneath the eaves of the Nicholson's house. It jittered and gave a jerk like it was out of sync with the world around it. Josh pointed it out to Marylis. It looked like a large melon in a garbage bag until it extended two squat legs as black as its body. It wobbled a couple steps forward, and a long neck uncoiled like a cobra readying to strike.

Josh could feel himself shaking, but he didn't seem to be able to move. The night, the woods, the house were gone. All he could see was that blacker-than-black thing. Just looking at it, he could feel its presence. It emanated…wrongness. Here was something more alien than any alien he'd ever seen on TV or in the movies, and it stood just a few feet above him in his reality. It bobbled up and down a few times, as if testing its legs. There was a swelling at the end of its neck, but that was as close as it got to having a head or a face. It had no eyes, no nose, no beak, no mouth.

Josh's knees were locked. He was sure he would have fallen down if they weren't. His field of vision had narrowed to such a degree that he wasn't even sure Marylis was still standing next to him. Forcing his arm to work, he raised it to see if she was. His fingers brushed her shoulder.

She screamed.

At that same instant, with a sound like an umbrella opening in an empty room, the thing from under the eaves extended two wings that seemed neither feathers nor skin. It shook them once and leapt from the roof. After catching an updraft, it flapped its wings, pushing itself higher into the darkening sky. Josh grabbed Marylis's arm without looking at her and pulled her through the trees towards Granma's house. With the express purpose of making sure they were running away from it, he struggled to keep the thing in view as he parted the vegetation in front of him with his free hand. It flew across the evening sky making the newly-emerging stars in its path wink out one after another.

6

Marylis looked as if her back were glued to the outside of Granma's front door.

Josh peeked up at the sky from behind one of the pillars.

Both were out of breath and wheezing.

"May-maybe it was just a raven," Josh said. "Yeah," this last encouragingly, he willed Marylis to agree with him as he moved to join her and leaned back against the door.

"THAT WAS NO BIRD!" she said. Reaching up she laid her hand gently on Max's head as if to make sure that the parakeet was still there.

He was pressing his tiny body as far as possible into her hair.

Well, Josh thought in a short flash of calm, *whatever we saw Max saw too, and he didn't like it any more than we did.*

The door behind them opened.

Both of them fell onto their backs on the floor of the entrance hall.

To save life and wing Max gave up hiding in Marylis's hair and fluttered to perch on the banister of the fake staircase.

"Hello, Marylis," Josh's mom said. She smiled and waved, as she stood bent over them. She turned her attention to Josh. "J, that little walk sure took a while."

He and Marylis stood up and started talking at once, "A-We-black thing-were in the-on the-bushes and-Nicholson's house." They stopped. Both took a breath.

Josh motioned for Marylis to go ahead.

"Mrs. Cotter," she started. "We were in the bushes looking for a frog over by the Nicholsons' and this big black thing with wings came swooping down at us."

"A bat?" Josh's mother said in that completely annoying aren't-we-over-reacting voice parents seem to enjoy using at every opportunity.

"No, Mom," Josh said shaking his head. "It wasn't a bat or a raven or any kind of bird. It was…it was…well it was something else is all, something wrong."

She looked at him and then at Marylis. "Well, I can tell you did see something."

Granma tromped in from the kitchen. "What's all the ruckus?"

Josh's mom kissed her on the cheek, "Nothing, Mom. Josh and Marylis just gave themselves a little fright."

Granma squinted at Josh. "What'd you see a ghost and she won't believe you?"

Josh opened his mouth, but he didn't get a chance to say anything.

His mother said, "Have a good night, Mom." She pushed him and Marylis toward the door. "Come on Marylis, I'll drive you home." She didn't wait for a response.

Josh looked over at Marylis helplessly.

She shrugged.

"Mom," Josh said as they were shepherded toward the car. "It was weird. It had a snake-neck and no face—no MOUTH! It wobbled on two stumpy legs!"

"Josh, I said I believe you saw something, but its no-face and snake-neck came more from the dark night and those cheap horror novels I've told you both not to read than it did from reality." She opened the car door for them, and they got in silently.

Just as his mom started the engine Marylis yelled, "MAX!"

Josh nearly jumped out of his socks. He was somewhat gratified to notice that his mom had jumped too.

"What?" his mother asked with her hand over her heart.

Marylis had already hopped from the car and was running toward the house.

"Her parakeet, Mom." he said. "She wears it in her hair sometimes, I guess."

"Remind me to tell her not to bring it to class." She took a deep breath. "And to ask her to never yell like that in my presence in the future."

Sometimes Josh thought his mom sounded too much like a parent. It was happening more and more often now that she was a teacher again. They not only had less time to have fun together, but she also seemed less capable of having fun.

Marylis came running back with Max in her hair. She sat down next to Josh, shut the car door, and stared at him expectantly.

He wondered what she expected him to do. His mother already considered the subject of the whatever-it-was closed.

"Marylis, he won't . . .dirty in the car will he?" Josh's mother asked.

Josh rolled his eyes. She said poop when they were alone, and they both laughed about it.

"No, ma'am." Marylis said.

His mother started driving, and Marylis gave her quiet directions from the back seat.

When they pulled up in front of her house, Marylis thanked Josh's mother. To Josh, she whispered, "We'll talk tomorrow."

He waved back when she waved from the curb. He wasn't sure he wanted to do anything at any point in his life that would remind him of what had happened tonight. To calm himself down, he listed the reasons he shouldn't "talk tomorrow": 1) forgetting that thing would make him a lot more comfortable, 2) Marylis is a girl AND a fifth grader, 3) he did not want to give Han Liss any more reasons to pound him, and 4) what did they have to talk about anyway? They'd seen a bat. That was all. Yeah.

He felt a tickle of fear, and couldn't keep his mind from adding, a great big bat with no eyes and no face.

All the way home he kept remembering a dull thud, a sound like an umbrella opening, and stars winking out, one by one.

7

"Will you please stop looking over my shoulder, PLEASE!" Marylis begged. "It is really annoying." They were standing in the hallway after school the next day. The hall was full of the echoey sounds of some of the teachers still working in their classrooms; most of the students were gone.

Josh grabbed one of her sleeves and dragged her over to the end of the locker bay where there was about a foot or two between the wall and the last locker. He squeezed himself into that small space. Now, anyone walking down the hall would probably only see Marylis since only his backpack stuck out into the hall. "I just don't want Han to see me talking to you," Josh said.

"You. Are. So. Whacked. How many times do I have to tell you that he could not care less who I talk to or what I do?"

"If he sees me talking to you it will remind him that I exist," Josh said.

Marylis shook her head. "Fine, I'll stand here and look like some uber-goombah who talks to lockers."

"I'm not chicken or anything," Josh said quickly. "There are three of them and just one of me. I don't—"

"I don't think you are chicken, okay?" She said angrily. "I'm his little sister, remember? I wouldn't be breathing today if I didn't hide from him sometimes."

"Not hiding," Josh said quickly. "Being stealthy."

With one eyebrow raised, Marylis stared at him over the rims of her glasses. There was silence between them for a moment.

"Well?" Josh said as if he were asking the time of day. "What did you want to talk about?"

Marylis pushed her glasses up her nose and glared at him for a moment. Hands on hips, she said sarcastically, "Bugs Bunny or Porky Pig who's the bigger ham? What do you think I want to talk about?" After a couple seconds of silence during which Josh looked everywhere but at Marylis, she practically shouted, "That black thing!"

When the echoes finally quieted and the last "-ing, ing, ing" gave way to silence once more, Josh said, "The bat?" doing his best to sound innocently convinced that it had been a bat.

"You know as well as I do that that was not a bat!" she said, adding an exclamation point to the end of her sentence with a stomp of her foot.

"So," Josh said pretending to find his shoelaces utterly fascinating. "I think we should agree that it was a bat and forget all about it."

Marylis started tapping her right foot. "It could be something dangerous." She said with quiet insistence.

"All the more reason to avoid it!" Josh countered still looking down.

"I thought you said you weren't chicken?" She sniffed the air between them sharply. "Well, I'm thinking I smell poultry!"

"It's not that." Josh could hear a note of whininess in his voice that made him decidedly uncomfortable. "I just think Mom was right. Nothing like that *could* exist. Whatever we saw had to have been augmented by our imaginations."

Marylis let loose an exasperated huff. "It was not our imaginations! How could it have been *augmented* by our imaginations in exactly the same way? We definitely saw the same thing. Josh, it could hurt someone if we ignore it."
Josh could feel her leaning toward him. He just knew her hands were still on her hips. Her foot began tapping faster.

"If it is dangerous," Josh said. "And it does hurt someone, I'd like to make sure that someone isn't us!" He realized he was still looking at his feet. He chanced a glance up at Marylis. She was smirking. *That is a look of disapproval if I ever saw one*, he winced and looked back at the ground.

"Look, I say we go out and try to find it." Marylis said sounding eminently sensible. "We're just looking. Remember, we got away from it easily enough last night. It didn't even seem to notice us." She took a deep breath. "We've got to see what it was! If it's a bat, so much for monster theories. But if it isn't a bat, we'll be heroes."

That hero part made Josh a little nervous. He didn't want to be a hero…too many of them seemed to come by that title only after they were dead or missing vital body parts. *If it does turn out to be something dangerous*, he told himself, *I could always convince Marylis that we need to go for help.* "Can we agree before we start that it's probably nothing?" he asked looking up at Marylis again.

She had a doubtful expression on her face, but then she shrugged. "I think we should do a little more research before we come to that conclusion."

It was probably just a very big raven that had…lost its beak and feathers somehow. No it was a bat…a slightly mutated—no deformed and nearly disabled bat. Josh made his decision. This was by far the most exciting thing that had happened to him since he'd left Dayton. There simply were no such things as monsters even here in Weirdsburg, USA. He would go along with Marylis and just pretend they were on a monster-finding mission. An imaginary adventure was better than going home to a stack of video and computer games he'd already beaten or a one-sided video chat with his Dayton friends. "Okay, let's go see what we can find," he sighed.

"Cool!" Marylis said. "I think we should wait until dusk to search for it."

"But I have to be at my Granma's for dinner at five," Josh said.

"Duh, Brainboy, I have to be home by five for dinner too." Marylis grabbed the front of his shirt and pulled until he gave up his hiding place. "We saw it just before nightfall last night. That's when we should look for it tonight—after dinner."

She started walking down the hall and Josh followed reluctantly. "So where are we going now?" He asked.

"Where does one go when one does research?" She asked sounding as if she were a teacher talking to a really slow-witted student.

Josh stopped walking. "Not the library!"

"What have you got against libraries?" She asked with another smirk.

"Nothing. I love libraries and books. It's the former and often substitute Town Librarian that gives me a pain."

Marylis rolled her eyes. "Well, is your grandmother substituting today?"

"Not that I know of."

"Well, put some hustle in your heinie! Time's a-wasting." Marylis motioned toward the door with her head causing her ponytail to make a complete revolution. "If she does happen to be there, we'll just play dodge-the-librarian while we research."

It is a cliché, Josh thought, but I am truly wondering: *What have I gotten myself into?*

8

The library was just one long block down Mine Street from the school. In any other town in America, Mine Street would have been called "Main." It ran right through the center of town and was home to all of the municipal buildings. There had never been a mine in or near Rock Hollow to cause the founding fathers to ignore this convention of Americana...Josh was sure they were just trying to prove their oddness. There was the post office, which resembled that pyramid on the back of a dollar bill. Why? Even Josh, with a lifetime of Granma's stories under his belt, had no earthly idea. It sat next to the town hall with its silver dome. Legend had it that the dome had been bronze or gold depending on who you talked to until lightning struck it and changed it to silver. People in town just looked at you funny if you asked what scientific principle would account for bronze turning into silver with the application of electricity. The rest of the street was lined with dark and creepy little storefront shops that had probably seen better days.

The library was the last building on the "business district" block of Mine Street. The block beyond the library was mostly residential with just a couple more storefronts. It was also home to Rock Hollow's only two restaurants, Muther's and the Chatter Box. Twin sisters who absolutely hated each other owned the competing diners. Josh had been to both a number of times during visits in past years, and a meal in one was indistinguishable from a meal in the other. The diners really had the same menu, but each had its own set of cutesy names for all the platters. "Toad in the Hole" at Muther's was the same as "Frog on a Log" at the Chatter Box, and both were just a fried egg in the cut-out center of a piece of toast. To satisfy his curiosity, Josh really wanted to ask Granma why the sisters couldn't stand each other to such a degree, but he was afraid that would get her going. Granma did not need story starters.

Josh and Marylis walked in silence. He figured Marylis was planning the whole monster hunt or maybe devising some research method to uncover information on imaginary devil bats. He was marveling at the fact that he and Marylis were...well, such good friends. He couldn't remember even thinking about being friends with a girl in Dayton. He was surprised that he was considering being...like best friends with one now, especially one in the fifth grade. For some reason though, he felt like he and Marylis had grown up together despite the fact that they had actually only met yesterday. It was pretty strange. *Well,* he thought to himself, *it may have something to do with the fact that she's the only person who's tried to be my friend*—He shut that thought off, but found you didn't need to complete a thought to feel its sting.

Marylis slowed a bit as they passed the post office.

Josh slowed to keep in step with her. She seemed to be mumbling to herself.

"Um, good day for a psychotic episode?" he asked. "Are you having a nice conversation with yourself?"

She stopped walking and, ignoring his snide questions, said, "I guess I should tell you...I mean it's only fair if you know everything I know. We won't find anything at the library today."

"What are you talking about?" He'd gone a step or two beyond her and had to turn around to look her in the eye. She looked completely normal. Josh wondered if there were outward signs of the onset of mental illness and what they looked like.

"I know how you're going to react to this, but I just wanted to tell you that I saw us finding out what that thing is. I mean exactly what it is and where it came from." She heaved a huge sigh. "Because of that, I know we won't find anything today at the library." She sounded certain and completely rational.

Josh just shook his head and said, "I repeat, what ARE you talking about?"

"See, ever since I was a baby, I've sorta been able to see the future."

Oh, boy, Josh thought, *oh-ho-ho, boy*. The Rock Hollow Crazy runs deep in this one..."Sorta?" He ventured.

"My visions take a little interpretation...see, I'm reverse psychic. If I see something happening, it definitely won't happen."

I can bolt right now, Josh thought. *When she comes to bang on Granma's door, I can pretend...I can...I can...I can run to one crazy person to save me from the first crazy person?* He realized they were just standing in the middle of the sidewalk, and he was silently staring at Marylis while he thought.

She made a face like she'd tasted something sour and said, "Okay, you're looking at me like I have three heads. Here's another example: night before last I had a dream and I saw us catching the perfect frog at Sand Street Pond last night."

"Saw as in had a vision?" Josh could hear the doubt in his own voice, and he could see she heard it too because her eyes were squinting, her brow was furrowing; her lips all but disappeared into a short tight line. "Bright lights, speaking in tongues, possible choirs of angels depending on your religious affiliation had-a-vision?"

"No tongues, no bright light, no angels," Marylis said evenly through that tiny moue of a mouth. "But yes, a vision. You and I stood next to the pond laughing and holding this humongous, slimy bullfrog."

"But we didn't catch a bullfrog," Josh said slowly. "And you knew we wouldn't because you'd seen us catch a bullfrog?"

"Right!" She said suddenly cheery. She started walking again. Over her shoulder she said, "You get it! See, reverse psychic. I have visions, they're just always opposite of what will actually happen."

Josh hesitated a second or two and then shrugged with one shoulder. *Okay, I can live with this. I live with Granma's stories. I live with having a science teacher who's a walking geek-timewarp. I live in a town where all the parents either make twist-ties or fake doggie doo. I...I can live with this.* He ran to catch up with Marylis.

The only strange thing about the library was that it was in Rock Hollow and there was nothing strange about it. It looked like a library, granite walls, white columns, two small but fierce looking lions flanking the front steps. It had been built in 1905. Mrs. Bauldridge, the first Town Librarian, had presided over the Rock Hollow Public Library for over fifty years. Josh's Granma took it over for the next forty, so Mrs. Picturtle, the current Town Librarian, was only the third person to hold that job.

Yet another pearl of historical trivia, Josh thought, *thanks to Granma and her stories.*

As they got to the top of the stairs, Josh stuck out his arm to block Marylis from entering the library and shushed her protest before it escaped her already open mouth.

He peeked through one of the small square windows. No one sat behind the main desk.

"What are you doing?" Marylis squeezed out between her clenched teeth.

"You want my help researching, right?" Josh asked quietly.

She nodded.

"Well, if Granma is behind that desk, and she sees me, she'll put me to work. Heck, she'll probably draft you too!"

Marylis rolled her eyes. "I've met your Grandmother. She's not unreasonable."

Josh smirked at her. "Relatives have a tendency to be a lot less reasonable when they are related to you."

"Whatever you say, Paranoia-lad."

Josh peered back into the comparative dimness of the library. Mrs. Picturtle's explosion of red, curly hair just visible over the circulation desk signaled the all-clear. He opened the door for Marylis and followed her in to begin their search.

9

Josh had to admit that he really liked being in old libraries. Not only were they guaranteed cool on a hot afternoon, but they were also full of crackle-paged books and the powdery, earthy scent of aging paper. His mom called that smell "musty." Josh always thought of it as the scent of knowledge.

He and Marylis sat at a dark, oak table large enough for a king's feast. Towers of thick green, canvas-covered books separated the two of them. The books held newspapers that dated back to the late 1800's. There were older papers, but only the librarians could get those for you. Josh worried that Granma had given Mrs. Picturtle permission to put him to work, and he didn't want to chance asking her for help.

The local history room felt almost alive. Josh thought he could sense its discomfort at the harsh fluorescent lights that buzzed softly above their heads, but without the long white bulbs the windowless room would be pitch black. The dark wooden shelves of leather bound books, each shelf with matching spines, and the two long wooden tables cried out to be lit with desk lamps under green glass hoods or even flutter-flamed gas lamps, not that Josh had ever seen a gas lamp anywhere outside a movie.

Only the occasional thunderous crinkle of aging newsprint pages being turned reminded Josh that Marylis was still across the book-mounded table from him. He would flip a page being careful not to man-handle it into disintegration and a moment later her turning of a page would fracture the silence. Then him again; they'd been at it for hours. Scanning every page of these silly, ancient newspapers was exhausting. He wondered if the brittle, old things would ever find their way into a computer file. That sure would make searching them a lot easier. It was nearing time for them to leave, and they hadn't found anything. He stood and stretched. "I guess you were right; we didn't find it."

Marylis stretched too. "Thanks for the sarcasm. But then I didn't expect you to believe me."

"I believe you. I believe you." He said. *Well, I can try to pretend I do*, he thought.

The two of them gathered up what they had brought with them and worked at getting it back into their bags.

"Well, *I* don't believe *you*," she said pulling on her backpack.

A thought struck him. "Wait, you said that if you see something happening, it definitely doesn't."

"Yes?" She said as they tromped up the stairs.

Over the jingly echo of the metal buckles on their packs, Josh said, "You said in your frog vision that you saw the two of us at the pond, but you didn't meet me until that night. If you saw me there, then something in your vision came true just as you saw it"

"Well, I didn't know the other person was Josh Cotter, my teacher's son." As they passed her, the both of them waved at Mrs. Picturtle, or at least her hair which was still all of her that was visible over the top of the desk. Josh didn't find it the least bit odd that the librarian's hand shot up to return the wave despite the fact that there was no way she could see them unless she had seeing-eye-hair.

Marylis continued, "There was just somebody else friendly with me at the pond. Haven't you ever spent time with someone in a dream that you knew in your dream but not in real life? It's like that." She opened the front door.

The brightness of the afternoon sun made both of them wince as they stepped outside. "I feel like a mole." Josh said blinking. "Please stop about your visions, though.

My brain hurts. I believe you, really." Josh was pretty sure he sounded truthful enough.

Marylis did not look convinced.

"One thing I did learn from all those newspapers and histories of Rock Hollow," Josh said as they descended the library steps. "Is that all of Gra—"

"What are you doin' with my sister?"

Josh did not even need to turn his head to know who had interrupted him.

"Buzz off, Hannibutt," Marylis said. "Or I'll frog you in your sleep tonight."

"Just you try, midget," Han said, his lips all snarly like a bad Elvis impersonator. He gave her a shove that sent her to the ground. Her head narrowly missed the pedestal of one of the lions.

She tried to get up, but Han pushed her back down with one enormous sneaker-clad foot.

At least, Han was Goon-less. Though even by himself, he was intimidating.

"I ast you a question," Han said stepping between the fallen Marylis and Josh.

"Just leave us alone," Josh said locking his knees to keep himself from backing away.

"I don't want no city crackers hanging around my sister," Hannibal said and took a long step toward Josh. The two of them were almost nose to nose, and Hannibal's breath was foul enough to kill a wombat.

Josh felt a heavy-hollow fear just behind his breast bone, but he stood his ground.

"Slime away, Creepybal," Marylis said coming around from behind her brother. She tried to squeeze in between them. "You don't want to make me mad."

"Aside from smelling like you just swallowed a garbage dump, what is your problem?" Josh said to Hannibal. "Marylis can hang out with whomever she wants."

"I'm gonna smash you flat," Hannibal said.

"Hi, Kids! Whatcha doing?" It was Granma, and she smacked Hannibal on the back as if they were old friends.

All three of them jumped, especially Hannibal. His eyes bugged out so far that it looked as if he'd been hit with a board in the back of the head.

Granma had come out of nowhere. Josh had been distracted, but she'd just sort of appeared. *Who knew Granma had mad ninja skills?* Josh thought.

"We—uh we were just talking," Hannibal said. His squinty eyes were darting all over the place trying to find an escape route. He inched away from Granma. Leaning close to Josh, he whispered through clenched teeth, "One day, just you wait." Then he trotted off down the sidewalk.

"You could use that boy's head for a whistle just by blowin' in one of his ears," Granma said. She looked down at Marylis. "Ooops, sorry. You're his sister, aren't you?"

"Since birth," Marylis said sarcastically. "Unfortunately."

"Marylis, this is my Granma Reece." Josh said.

"I told you, Goober," Marylis said to Josh. "I've met your Grandmother." They shook hands anyway.

Josh shrugged. "What are you doing here, Granma?"

"Saving you from Bully-boy not reason enough?"

"Granma!" Josh felt his cheeks heat and knew he was blushing. His mother would say Granma was "frank." To Josh that just meant "embarrassing in most social situations."

"I'm here to pick up my check for the last time I worked for Ardatha."

It took Josh a second to realize that she meant Mrs. Picturtle. "Oh."

"I should probably go," Marylis said jerking her thumb over her shoulder at her retreating brother. "Jabba-the-butt would just love it if I got punished for being late to dinner. I'll meet you at your Granma's in an hour or so, Josh."

They said their good-byes and nice-to-see-yous, and Marylis left.

"Nice girl, Josh-B'gosh," Granma said. She winked at him.

"Please don't call me that. I just met her yesterday. We aren't dating or anything."

Granma laughed. "Maybe someday, though, right?" She laughed again, and it sounded like a crow with asthma.

Josh just shook his head, and followed her back inside the library to wait while she picked up her check.

10

Just before seven, Josh and Marylis sat on the curb in front of Granma's house.

"We must have missed it," Marylis said.

"We looked under the eaves of all the houses in a three street radius!" Josh said. "We checked every tree big enough for it to hide in. We did the best that we could short of dragging a ladder around for a chimney check." He had to admit he was relieved they hadn't found anything. He also had to admit that the thrill of the hunt had made for a fun evening's adventure.

Marylis reached to touch her unoccupied ponytail. "I should have brought Max. He always brings me good luck."

"We may have had good luck not finding it." Josh said staring into the street. "Maybe the only reason it didn't viciously devour us last night was that it didn't see us."

Marylis stood. "Come on," she pulled him up. "It's just now starting to dusk. Is that a verb? I'm not allowed to stay out after dark." They walked between the two houses across the street. "We really only have about a half hour before we enter the danger zone. No later than 7:30 or my parents will kill me."

They passed the pond and the Nicholsons and then crossed Granite Street. The sun was just visible over the western ridge of the hollow. Everything was sharply outlined but yellowy in the intense evening light. Josh thought it looked like a scene that was supposed to appear "historical" in a bad TV movie. They half-slid, half-walked down a hill to a tiny creek. The water was only about two or three feet across and not more than a few inches deep. There were greeny-brown fluffy looking plants swaying in the currents. A rainbow patch of gasoline floated by followed by some water bugs that Josh's dad called Water Striders. "Any snakes?" Josh asked hearing the hint of unease in his own voice.

"No such luck," Marylis answered. "Just imagine how high I could get Han to jump with a nice wet snake in his drawers!"

They both laughed.

"Does this creek have a name?" Josh asked.

Marylis looked at the brownish water for a moment. "Not really. It's just a run-off ditch. When it rains, water from the storm drains runs down here through pipes. We just call it 'the creek'."

"Creative," Josh said with more than a little sarcasm.

"HEY!" Marylis jumped in the air. "I got it! I know where we didn't look."

Josh tried to suppress a shiver.

"Follow me," She tromped off down the creek away from the Nicholsons and Granma's.

While he wondered why he suddenly felt like shivering, he said, "Did you just have a vision?"

"No, Idjit, I can't have them on demand. I just thought of a place to look."

They passed one more house.

"Where?" he asked jogging to keep up.

He smelled it before she could answer his question. A wet, green algae smell that was much stronger than the earthy-metal scent of the creek itself. He'd been watching his feet trying not to step in the water, so he had to look up. A huge concrete tunnel jutted out of the hill beneath Quartz street. Algae hung in the water pouring out of it like some stringy, green beard. The tunnel itself was very dark with no end in sight. Josh felt cool air against his skin as if the tunnel were exhaling on them. "Where does it come out?" He asked.

"Well it 'comes out' here," Marylis said pointing to the water pouring from the pipe.

Josh gave her an "over-the-glasses" look despite the fact that he wasn't wearing glasses.

"It starts on the other side of the park."

"Down by your house," Josh said.

"Yep. Han says he's walked all the way through it, but he's so scared of slimy things. I don't believe a word of it. I think he's even afraid of algae."

Josh rubbed at his arms where the cool corpse breath of the tunnel had given him goosebumps. "This is where you think that thing is?"

"It's just a guess." She shrugged. "It was hiding in a dark place yesterday up on the Nicholsons' roof . . .I just thought—"

"It's definitely dark in there," Josh finished.

Marylis nodded.

"Listen," Josh said. They heard the trickle of water and beneath that a dull roar that sounded like the ocean. "What's that?" He whispered.

"Like a seashell, I guess," Marylis whispered back.

"No, not the roaring sound. That trickle." Josh said.

"Back in there a ways there are—" Marylis searched for the right word. "Tributary tunnels that run into this big one—"

SPLASH! Came from not too far back in the tunnel.

Marylis grabbed Josh's arm.

They had time to exchange a glance, before... THWUMP! Like an umbrella opening.

The black thing burst from the tunnel and flew directly at them.

Marylis screamed.

11

Josh grabbed Marylis with both hands. He threw himself to the ground, and dragged her with him. The fall seemed to take hours. It couldn't have been long though, because in two wing-beats, the space of one heartbeat, the length of half a breath, the black thing swooped just over them where they lay in the creek.

Josh forced his eyes to stay open. There was no chance of their getting away from it, so he had to see it. If it was going to get them no matter what, attack them, maybe kill them; he was going to do everything he could to understand what it was. He might even be able to fend it off somehow.

Its surface wasn't feathers or fur. It wasn't scales or amphibious slime. It looked cool and smooth like metal or maybe dark, discolored, dry dolphin's skin. He had the crazy idea that if he tried to touch it, his hand would vanish into it and be gone forever. He let go of Marylis and jammed both his hands beneath his back to keep himself from trying it.

The black thing didn't seem to notice them lying in the puddled water under the mouth of the tunnel. As soon as it was properly air born and far enough away, Josh jumped up and pulled Marylis after him.

"What are you doing?" She nearly screamed trying to wrest her arm from his grasp.

"I'm following it. We—"

"You're WHAT!? It almost got us, and you want to follow it?" She kept twisting left and right trying to loosen his hold on her.

"We have to see where it goes, and what it does." He was breathing hard from fright and the effort of pulling her along behind him, but he kept moving in the direction the thing had flown. "You said yourself we have to do 'further research.' Well, the library was a bust. We've got to have some facts. Remember what happened when we went to my mother with just the story that we'd seen it? No adult is going to believe us unless we have proof or at the very least more information."

She stopped resisting, and began to follow. "Okay, we chase it, but we don't have to go near it, right?"

If he weren't so scared that he felt his heart beating right at the back of his throat, Josh would have laughed at this complete role reversal. Now he wanted to go after the

71

thing, and she was urging caution. However, he was sure that one laugh would send him down the slippery slope of insanity and straight into the giggle academy.

Careful to keep the flapping, black thing in sight, Josh climbed the hill on the opposite bank of the creek. "No we don't have to go near it," he finally answered. "If it just flies out into uninhabited woods and eats some bugs or something, who cares how scary it looks? But if it —does something...something else—" He didn't want to think of the horrible things something that...out of place might do. He didn't finish his sentence, and he tried to force his imagination not to complete the thought in pictures. As luck would have it, his misbehaving mind supplied the image of the creature embracing a person with its leathery wings and seconds later only bones falling at its feet...he imagined the top of its blub head opening on a hinge to display a shark's nightmare of teeth.

It flew out over the park. The two of them followed dodging trees and culverts and tree roots while attempting to keep an open patch of sky above their heads. As they ran, they did their best to keep behind it and out of its line of sight...if it had a line of sight.

"It's not flying toward uninhabited woods," Marylis said.

Josh nodded. "Your house sorta," he huffed.

They jumped the low park fence and ran down Silver Street.

As the sky got darker, it got harder to follow. They had to track the winking of the stars.

"I think it has stopped flying," Josh quit running and tried to catch his breath. "Is it circling?" He made an attempt to point, but he was so out of breath that his hand only made it half way up. He flapped it a couple of times in the direction the thing had flown. "What's in those trees?"

"Two houses," Marylis said as she pulled up beside him.

A driveway disappeared between the trunks of trees whose branches nearly obscured the sky. Because of the dense foliage, they hadn't seen the thing land. As they approached the driveway, Josh wondered if it was lurking in the branches of one of the trees waiting to drop down on them. He felt like a cartoon character caught in the shadow of a descending piano. He shook his head. "Does anyone live out there?"

"One is used by some rich people from Cincinnati as a sort of Summer house," Marylis said. "The other belongs to crazy Miss McGwinnon."

Josh paused to wonder what you had to do in this town to be called "crazy."

They crept up the gravel drive. Both of them stepped carefully on the loose stones and kept a close eye on what they could see of the sky and the over-hanging tree branches.

"There it is!" Josh pointed. It hadn't landed yet; it seemed to be circling above one of the houses. As they watched, it made one more complete circle before descending toward the roof.

"That's Miss McGwinnon's," Marylis said in a husky whisper.

"Maybe it's just looking for a place to sleep tomorrow," Josh raised his eyebrows hopefully. "Maybe it ate all it needed to while it was flying or something."

Marylis shrugged. Her hair bushed out around her face like a windblown patch of weeds and her eyes filled the frames of her glasses. Her lips, even in the twilight, looked slightly blue from the chill. The rest of her looked like she'd lost a water-balloon fight in a pigpen.

She looks as scared as I feel, Josh thought. The night air, blowing over his own creek-water-soaked clothes, made his teeth chatter. Even though he was certain Marylis knew he was scared, he hoped she didn't think he was such a fraidy cat that his teeth were clickety-clicking out of fear.

The thing landed on the roof of Miss McGwinnon's house. Josh and Marylis stared up at it from behind the trunk of a leafless, dead maple tree. The thing hobbled across the roof, bobbing up and down. It moved like a chimp with a limp. At an open window, it balanced on one clawed foot and pulled the screen out with the other. Two quick hops to the edge of the roof and it dropped the screen over the side. Josh watched it sail, swinging in arc after arc down to the grass. He looked up just in time to see the black thing vanish into the dark rectangle of the now completely open window.

The two of them stared at each other for a moment.

"Well," Josh said. "What does Miss McGwinnon do that's so 'crazy'?"

"Nothing really. There was the peanut butter incident, but—"

"The what?" Josh said.

Marylis waved at the air as if dismissing the whole story. "She bought all the peanut butter in town and then laid in a bathtub full of it in her back yard every day one summer until the neighbors complained. Other than that, she's just 'crazy' because she hates everyone. She used to have about a hundred cats until the town made her get rid of them."

"Maybe she's a witch and the black thing is her new pet. You know, like she conjured it..." He immediately felt like an idiot. Everyone knew witches weren't real, at least not that stuff about old ladies in black with broom fixations. *Well*, said a quiet, little voice in his head, *black bat-birds that sleep in dark, creepy crevices aren't real either, are they?*

They sneaked up to a lighted, downstairs window. Inside, an old woman, who looked like she could easily win a roll in a movie about those broom-loving old ladies, sat in a big chair watching TV and feeding sardines to a cat roughly half the size of Rhode Island.

Josh and Marylis looked at each other again.

"Well?" mouthed Marylis.

Suddenly, Miss McGwinnon's cat stood up and hissed loud enough for them to hear it over the television and through the closed window. Ignoring the next sardine that she'd been dangling in front of it, the cat leapt from her lap and ran out of sight.

The thing came down the stairs quicker than Josh would have thought its drunken monkey gait would permit. He started to yell, but what happened next, happened much too fast.

Miss McGwinnon called to her cat. She pushed off both arms of her chair with her knobbley hands and turned. She saw the thing, and she screamed.

The black thing launched itself at her.

Marylis grabbed Josh's arm. Her fingers dug into his bicep.

Flapping its wings slowly to hold itself steady, the thing latched on to one of the old lady's arms with each of its taloned feet. It hung its tiny melon head directly in front of her face. A ray of misty light appeared between Miss McGwinnon's face and the thing's head.

In a moment, she stopped struggling. In another moment, she slumped to the floor.

12

Josh grabbed Marylis's hand and pulled her down the driveway. They didn't stop running until they reached Marylis's front porch. It seemed frighteningly close to whatever they had just witnessed, but the distance and the familiarity such as it was engendered a not insignificant feeling of safety. Both of them nearly collapsed on to the steps.

Josh wheezed and puffed trying to talk. Finally he managed, "Ca—can't deny it exists now. Wha—What do you think it did to her?"

Marylis just shook her head without looking up.

"We've got to tell someone now," Josh said.

"Who?" Marylis squeezed out between gusts of breath.

Josh just stared in the direction of Miss McGwinnon's house. It was really no darker out than it had been a few moments ago, but the woods lining the edges of Silver and Marble Streets felt closer and more sinister. The branches of the trees seemed like upturned roots drawing night down to the earth. Maybe it wasn't the trees so much as the blackness between them. In a world where web-winged things flew at dusk, who knew what might hide in that blackness?

"I say," Marylis said. "That we go talk to the sheriff."

Josh wrinkled his nose and let out a short cough of a laugh.

"What?" Marylis nearly shouted. "She might be dead."

"Pretend you're the sheriff," Josh said. "What would you say if two kids came into your office and said 'We saw a black thing suck light out of an old lady's head' Huh?"

"All right, all right," Marylis patted at the air with the palms of both hands. She stared at the ground, her eyes moving rapidly back and forth. "So it's not the greatest idea in the world."

"Well, the sheriff might listen once we took him to the house, but I don't think so." Josh rubbed at his head. "I don't know the sheriff, but I bet we couldn't even get him to go there with us." He kept seeing that thing and the smoky ray of light between it and Miss McGwinnon. Even as he swept it away from in front of his mind's eye, the image came back clear as ever. "Would anyone in your family listen to us?"

"Josh," she looked up at him. "I know you don't know them, so I won't laugh. Hannibal is pretty much the nicest person in my family except my grandmother, and she can't help us."

"Okay," Josh said. "I'll talk to my mom. She always says to come to her if I need to talk about anything."

"She'll think you're joking," Marylis shook her head.

"No she'll think I'm telling wild stories to get her to move out of Rock Hollow."

Marylis looked confused. "Why would you want to do that?"

"Opera singing neighbors. Granma's house looks like a tomb. Post Office is a pyramid. Strange stories about stranger relatives. Everything named after some rock or a metal or a mineral. This is a weird town."

She smiled. "Yeah, but it's really no weirder than—"

Something roared from within the house.

It startled them both.

"Uhoh." Marylis tapped her bare wrist.

Josh looked at his watch and cringed. "8:16."

"MARYLIS ELIZABETH LISS WHERE HAVE YOU BEEN?"

Josh felt the porch shake with each syllable.

"We'll-talk-tomorrow-at-school," Marylis said in such a rush that it sounded like one word.

She scurried up the steps and into the blackness beyond the door.

Josh didn't know what to do. As long as that thing was out there, he knew he wouldn't sleep even with his window locked.

His mom would listen. She had to.

He looked out across the wide-open field at the south end of the park. A run across it and through the woods at the north end was the quickest way to Granma's house, but it was so dark. The black thing could descend on him from out of the night sky or from the branches of any of the trees. In that pesky mind's eye of his, he could see it swooping down on him for a little dessert after a hearty meal of old lady.

He shook the picture out of his head. All he had to do was make it back to Granma's. Josh looked up at the black sky, clenched his teeth, and ran off into the night.

13

Josh dashed up Sand Street.

He kept looking over his shoulder. It did nothing to make him feel any better.

He knew the thing was out there. He could feel it at his back whenever he faced forward. In his mind he saw its faceless head flying directly toward him like some black missile from out of the shadows, saw its talons reaching for his arms. He now understood the phrase "makes your flesh crawl." He felt as if his shirt were made of agitated insects.

When he turned around to look, he was never sure he hadn't seen it. Was that the normal twinkling of the stars or the black thing obscuring them as it flew? Was that only a branch swinging across the moon or something unnatural swooping toward him? Still, he could never convince himself he had seen it, and some small part of his mind was thankful for that.

It seemed to take days, or rather nights, but he finally reached Granma's porch.

He looked over his shoulder one more time as he reached to open the door. The doorknob flew out of his hand.

"Joshua Anthony Cotter where have you been?"

He jumped, lost his footing, and fell right at his mother's feet for the second time in as many nights.

"Well?" She paused.

Did she really expect him to answer her from the floor? Wasn't she going to offer him a hand up?

She leaned a little closer to him. "It is nearly nine. You have been gone for three hours."

"Mom, I've got to talk to you." He stood up and dusted himself off.

"I'll say you do, young man," she said in that other annoying parent voice: the you-have-just-stated-the-obvious-Buster voice.

Josh grabbed the inside doorknob that was still in his mother's hand and slammed the door behind him.

"Jah-ah-ahsh!" She said his name as if it had three syllables.

"Mom, you don't know what's out there. Marylis and I saw it again. We saw what it does!"

"Joshua what are you talking about? You aren't going to get out of this by acting like a loon. You really had me worried." She crossed her arms.

"That thing we saw yesterday. It's not feathers or fur. We found it again, and we followed it. We followed that black thing. It really has no face, and it got her. We were looking in the tunnel on the creek—"

"Josh, calm down." Even though he was nearly as tall as his mother, she was slouching down slightly as if she were talking to a little kid.

He realized he was thinking and saying things out of order. The rush of relief at being inside, being out from beneath that sky and away from whatever might be floating around in it mixed the events of the day around in his head. It felt as if all the air around him had vanished. His thoughts kept leaping out of reach. His mouth felt broken.

"Okay," she said placing a hand on his shoulder. "You went looking for that bat you saw—"

Everything spun into focus around the word "bat." "Mom, it's not a bat. Bats don't have long necks and sharp claws. We found it in the tunnel and we followed it. We think it killed someone—"

"What?" She said as much an exclamation as a question. She looked confused and tired. She stepped back.

"Yes, we saw it grab her and suck the life out of her. It—"

"Joshua, that's enough. You know I don't like it when you lie." She was standing up straight again with her hands on her hips.

Trying to keep any traces of whine out of his voice, trying to sound calm and rational despite his fear and confusion, Josh said, "Mom, I'm not--"

"I said enough. I know you don't like it here in Rock Hollow, but that's no reason for you to make up silly stories. I thought we talked and were honest about how we felt in this family."

"What family?" The words were out of his mouth before he could stop them. Josh was immediately sorry he'd let them escape. He certainly didn't mean it.

She blinked three times, and said quietly, "Not one more word. March into the kitchen and kiss your Grandmother. We are leaving."

His stomach jumped. His throat was as raw as if he'd just thrown up. He had to say something but couldn't think what. He wanted to apologize. But he also wanted to say Miss McGwinnon's name, so that when they found her tomorrow or whenever, he might be able to win back his mom's attention.

Before he could even open his mouth, she said, "MARCH!" She pointed toward the back of the house.

Granma was waiting for him at the window to the kitchen. She put her finger to her mouth and shook her head. Leaning through the window, she hugged him and kissed his cheek. She pressed a small piece of paper into his hand just before patting him on the back, propelling him back toward the front door.

The intensity of his mother's angry reaction to his thoughtless words and the whole horror film of a night had thrown everything back into a confusing swirl. Josh didn't even see the paper as he shoved it into his jeans pocket and followed his mother out to the car.

Once they'd gotten in, she held up one hand like a traffic cop and without looking back at him said, "Not one word. You have really cheesed me off, Joshua Anthony. We will talk about your behavior tomorrow."

Josh hoped they would both be around tomorrow. As long as the thing only fed...or whatever...once a night everyone else in town would be safe for one more day at least. As long as there was only one of them...that thought sent fresh shivers through his whole body. If only his mother had only let him finish a sentence, he was sure he could have said something that would have made her listen.

Then he had to open his big mouth and say the one thing that would guarantee punishment. Something close to how he sometimes felt; and, he knew, exactly what his mother feared he always felt. But he didn't think they weren't a family, and now he couldn't get her to listen to him about his real feelings or that black thing out there in the night without making her angrier.

On the way home, he just kept playing the run to Granma's over and over in his mind. It brought that bugs-on-his-back certainty that the thing was going to swoop down on him, but it kept his mind off the fight with his mother.

Josh decided once his mom was asleep, he'd make the rounds of the house and check that all the windows were closed tightly and locked. He also planned to leave his light on all night. Turning it out would only feed the shadows.

14

Early the next morning, Josh sat up in bed. He did not want to go down stairs. In fact, he did not even want to be in his life at this moment. His fear and anger and frustration had kept him up. Once, his father had let him drink a whole cup of coffee. It had been gross and bitter even with tons of milk and sugar. For most of the rest of that day, Josh had felt like he was vibrating, like every part of his body, inside and out, was in constant motion. That was exactly how he'd felt all night. He hadn't fallen asleep until after two a.m. He was more tired than he could ever remember being. It felt like someone had taken a blow dryer to his brain and the inside of his stomach.

He got up and pulled on his favorite T-shirt and the jeans he'd worn yesterday. If he was going to have to face a horrible day, he wanted to be extra comfortable.

His mom had never been this angry with him. He didn't know what to expect.

"Well," he whispered to his reflection in his dresser mirror as he chased his bed-head away with his brush. "Let's just get it over with."

On the way down to breakfast, he decided on a course of action. He wouldn't say anything about the black thing, nor would he apologize for what had really made his mom angry last night. He would say Miss McGwinnon's name, and that was all. Even when his mom asked him why he'd said it, he'd just say "Nothing, just Miss McGwinnon." Then when they found that poor old lady, he'd use the fact that he'd said her name before anyone knew anything was wrong to get his mom to listen to him. Miss McGwinnon lived alone. Her nearest neighbors were gone for the winter. It really seemed that no one wanted anything to do with her. Chances were good that no one had found her yet.

He heard the radio or the television talking news from the kitchen. Josh peeked around the edge of the door. His mother was clearing some papers she'd been grading from the table in preparation for breakfast.

Slowly, he walked into the kitchen. "Miss McGwinnon," he said firmly.

His mom turned down the radio. "Did you have the radio on upstairs too? Isn't that so sad? All alone and having a stroke like that. She could have died out there in that isolated house of hers. They wouldn't have found her for days, maybe weeks, if it hadn't been for that anonymous tip." She set two cereal bowls on the table.

Josh had already opened his mouth to say "Nothing, just Miss McGwinnon," but he hadn't started speaking. He stood with his mouth hanging open for a moment. His thoughts buzzed randomly around his head like airsick bees. Finally he said, "What anonymous tip?"

"Didn't you hear that part? That's why it was on the radio. Late last night someone called the sheriff and said something horrible had happened to Miss McGwinnon. At first they thought it was a crank, but they have to follow up all their calls. Even the police don't knock on crazy Miss McGwinnon's door without a good reason. They found her on her living room floor. She'd had a massive stroke. Now they're looking for the person who called. They are afraid she was robbed too since one of the screens was ripped out...but they really couldn't tell if anything was taken given the way she kept house." She turned up her nose at, Josh guessed, the description of the place from the radio.

His mother set a plate of toast in the center of the table. She put the healthy cereal and the good cereal boxes next the milk and pulled out a chair for each of them.

"Josh," she said finally looking directly at him. "I need to apologize for getting so angry last night."

They both sat down. His mom stared at him for a moment. Josh stared through her trying to understand all she'd just said. He'd expected more anger or maybe quiet disapproval but not an apology. And what about Miss McGwinnon?

She reached out for his hand and said, "I was really worried when you didn't come back by eight. Then your grandmother and I had an argument about your father and money and us moving into that bizarre house of hers. I'm afraid I took it out on you." She squeezed his hand. "So, J, I'm sorry."

Josh stared at her. After a minute or so of silence, he half-smiled, nodded, and said, "I'm sorry too. I really, really didn't mean what I said that made you so mad. My mouth just moves before my brain can stop it sometimes."

She smiled, "So long as it's 'sometimes' and not 'often.' And I was already mad when you fell through the door. What do you say, mutual kick in the kiester for us thoughtless peoples?" She raised her eyebrows.

Josh smiled and nodded. "Boot!" they said at the same time, each kicking at imaginary kiesters under the table. *Now this feels like old times*, he thought, his smile broadening.

As they both started eating, his mother paused looking confused for a moment. "Now, what were you going to say about Miss McGwinnon?" she asked. "I didn't know you knew who she was?"

He realized that, for a moment, he'd forgotten all about that black monster whatsis. At that same instant, the obvious struck him. If he hadn't been worried about the argument with his mom he'd have thought of it right away. "Marylis!" Josh said out loud. Marylis had to be the anonymous tipper.

"Oh, they do live close to each other," his mother said mistaking what he'd said for an answer to her question which was just as well.

She went on talking, telling old stories about crazy Miss McGwinnon, but Josh was only listening enough to know when to nod. As he ate his cereal, he wondered why Marylis had called the sheriff. All his plans to get his mother on their side were useless now. He wanted to kick himself for real for what he'd said to his mother and kick himself again for not having the presence of mind to just go ahead and blurt out Miss McGwinnon's name last night no matter how mad it would have made his mom.

What could he and Marylis do to get help now? He had to talk to her. Pronto!

15

"I guess I understand why—" Josh started.

"What do you mean 'you guess'? Miss McGwinnon was lying there on her floor. She could have been dying. She could have been dead. We had no idea what it did to her." Marylis swung her hands through the air as if she were playing some mysterious string game without the string. "We couldn't very well leave her until someone missed her. That could have been months! Twenty percent of the town has forgotten she's out there and the other eighty per cent are either scared of her or count it as a good day when they don't have to deal with another 'incident.'"

At Josh's insistence they had sneaked out of the cafeteria during lunch to get some privacy and to hide from Hannibal. They ate at the bottom of the stairwell underneath the stairs as they discussed their situation.

"Okay," Josh said. "Okay. You're right. I'm just depressed because we can't use our advance knowledge of what happened to Miss McGwinnon to get my mom to help like I'd planned." Josh took a bite and chewed for a moment. "Why didn't you tell the police the whole story?"

Marylis stopped chewing and raised one eyebrow. "You said yourself they wouldn't believe us. Even your mom didn't believe you. Besides I was sneaking out of my room and out of my house to use a pay phone in the middle of the night after being sent to my room for major rule breaking. I was worrying more about being caught than about what I should say."

"You used a pay phone?" Josh said incredulously. "Who knew they even existed anymore?"

"Of course they still exist. And of course I used a pay phone! Hello," Marylis waved a hand in front of his eyes as if he were blind. "Calling 911. They trace every call."

"Okay, sheesh! Sorry. I don't call the police every day! I've never called the police!" After a minute, Josh said, "So, what next?"

"I have yet to thank you for getting me soaked in stinky creek water yesterday. Because of that and because I was out way late, I am being royally punished."

"This thing has killed." Josh shook his sandwich at her. "It may kill again, and you're complaining about being punished?"

"Number one, you're the one who was willing to leave Miss McGwinnon lying there. Number two she isn't dead. You said you heard the radio report. Did you listen? They think she had a massive stroke. She's in the hospital with two other 'stroke victims.'" Marylis scraped a lettuce chunk from Josh's sandwich off her lap. "And number three, the only creativity my mother displays is in coming up with really evil punishments." She paused and blinked as if she were trying to keep from crying. "I have to clean the bathroom."

"I didn't hear the radio report. My mom told me about it. And so what if you have to clean the bathroom? I do every other month at my house."

"Josh, this is the bathroom Hannibal uses."

"Ooo," Josh said scrunching up his face.

"Right." She nodded.

"Two others?" Josh asked letting his eyes unfocus as he stared at the floor.

"Yeah. Scary, old Mr. Mikaplike and poor, silly Mr. Prescot."

They sat in silence a moment. Both of them stared at what they were eating without seeing it. Josh couldn't taste his either. He had a dried-out, manky feeling in his mouth and everything tasted like spit and sand.

Marylis was the first to speak, "So to answer your question of so long ago: I don't know what next."

"Maybe it didn't hurt her. Maybe it was just looking at her and she really did have a stroke because—" Josh stopped. Marylis was giving him an evil look. "Okay, stupid line of thought." Josh stared at the empty baggies in his lap. "I'm afraid to bring up the whole monster thing with Mom again, so she's out. If my mother won't help us, we're certainly not going to get help from a stranger." He had explained to Marylis about his misfiring mouth last night and making up with his mother this morning.

Marylis looked at her watch. "We're going to be late."

Josh shrugged. "If we don't think of something to do, we could end up being monster lunch any night."

"Way to show that positive attitude!" Marylis said.

They cleaned up their lunches and tossed the bags into a trash barrel.

"How about you call me tonight after you clean the bathroom?" Josh reached in his jeans pocket to get his pen. When he pulled the pen out, a small wad of paper flipped out as well and skittered across the floor. He stared at it for a minute.

"What's that?" Marylis asked.

At first, Josh honestly did not know. Then he remembered. "Granma gave it to me last night after I ran in yelling about the monster. I forgot all about it because of my fight with Mom."

"What's it say?"

"I don't know," he said with a half shrug. "I didn't read it. I was a little preoccupied. I just stuffed it in my pocket."

"Well, you can read it now!"

"Yeah. Why are you so antsy? My Granma does dumb things sometimes. It's probably a recipe or maybe the title of a book she thinks I would like."

"Read. Read!"

"Okay!" He opened it up. Marylis stood on tiptoe to look over his shoulder.

The note read:

> Josh,
>
> I know what it was you saw. Bring your
> little friend over tomorrow after school.
> Be careful. The Shadowangel has returned.
>
> -Granma

"Wonderful," Josh said.

"'Little friend' is kind of insulting, but why do you sound so sarcastic?" Marylis said. "She's an adult, and it sounds like she is going to help us."

"Marylis, my Granma is a little loony. She's always making up stories—"

"We are wicked late." Marylis interrupted. She dashed up the stairs. Pausing one flight up to lean over the railing, "Meet me after school. I've always wanted to see the inside of your Granma's house!"

She was gone.

Josh just rolled his eyes. If Granma is the best help we can get, he thought, we might as well just resign ourselves to being eaten.

16

"So how do you think she knows what we saw?" Marylis asked as they walked down Mine Street towards her house. She had insisted they stop there to pick up Max before going to his Granma's even though it was completely out of the way.

"I don't know," Josh said, annoyed with the whole idea of going to his Granma for help. "I really doubt she knows anything."

"It sure sounded like she did from that note." Marylis did a little shiver that had to be exaggerated if it wasn't completely pretend. "Oooo, shadowangel isn't that the perfect name for it? I can't wait to find out everything."

Josh dropped his backpack on the sidewalk and stopped walking. "You are a total freak. This is a monster we're talking about. If you're so anxious to find out what she knows why do we have to go pick up your dang parakeet?"

Marylis rolled her eyes. "Number one: he's always been good luck for me, remember?" She reached out and tried to pull Josh around the corner on to Marble Street. "Number two: he's missed enough of this adventure already." She gave his arm one last yank and started walking backwards across her neighbor's lawn while still talking. "And number three: answer my question. How do you think she knows what we saw?"

"Will you please stop talking in numbered lists it's a really annoying habit," He said grabbing the strap of his pack and following her across the grass. "I'm sure she doesn't know anything. Granma likes to be the center of attention. If she tells us anything today, it'll just be something she's made up."

"She wasn't making up the Nicholsons," Marylis said matter-of-factly.

"I know." They had reached Marylis's front porch. Josh grimaced trying to keep that mind's eye of his firmly shut against images of the events of the previous evening. "But she makes up most things she talks about."

"Like what?" Marylis asked.

"Are you sure you want to go in there?" He indicated her front door with a flick of his wrist. "Won't you get in trouble for not cleaning the bathroom if someone sees you?"

"No, I can do it any time this week." Marylis said. She glared at him for a moment. "Wait here." She sounded fed up.

She was back in less than a minute with Max perched at the base of her ponytail.

He looked bright-eyed and, Josh thought, like most birds, more than slightly lizardy especially around his eyes.

"Okay, stop trying to change the subject," Marylis said as they started off across the park. "Your Granma makes up things like what?"

Josh shrugged. It was really embarrassing to let people know exactly how loopy his Granma was. "Well," Josh sighed giving in. Marylis was sure to find out sooner or later if they spent any time together. "Granma mostly makes up wild stories about the family. Sometimes she makes up weird stories about the town or people in it. Weird stories that can't be true...in any universe, really."

"LIKE WHAT?"

It didn't seem she was going to let him get away without telling her one of Granma's embarrassing whoppers. He thought for a second trying to find one that wasn't too outlandishly strange, but they all were. He just picked one. "Like, she says my Great Grand Uncle Percy had a third eye—"

"In the back of his head." Marylis finished for him as if she were supplying Uncle Percy's hair color or the fact that he worked at the corner store.

"What! Has she been blabbing these stories all over town?" Josh nearly screamed. He was suddenly horrified…storytelling at the library? A column in the local paper?

"No," Marylis said. "Your Uncle Percy used to wear a bobby pin on either side of his third eye to hold the hair out of the way." As she walked she pretended to move her hair from in front of an imaginary eye in the back of her own head. Max didn't seem to mind. He hopped onto one of her hands and continued to stare at Josh with birdy curiosity.

Josh stopped again. He stood in the middle of the sidewalk shaking his head.

Marylis stopped too and turned around. She quit patting Max on the head long enough to shrug. "I never saw him or even any pictures, but everyone knew about his extra eye. He used to run the general store up on Mine Street. All our grandparents and great-grandparents knew not to try shoplifting in that store. Even when his back--"

"Cut it out. Cut it out," Josh said haltingly. "I don't believe you." Actually, he needed to not believe her. If he did, he'd have to reconsider believing in Cousin Cisa's gills,

Great-great Grammy Theresa Reece's wings, Great-great-great Granpa Macy Reece's knack for levitation… There were too many strange stories he'd been told over his lifetime. It was too much. Nobody had that kind of a freak show for a family.

"Ask anyone," Marylis said putting Max back on her ponytail.

"I will," Josh said angrily even though he knew he wouldn't. She was still pretty much the only person in town he'd talked with. Every other conversation he had with people in Rock Hollow went like this: Them: "You're a Reece, aren't you?" Josh: "Yes." Them: "I knew it the moment I saw you." Smile. Smile. If any, let alone all, of Granma's stories about the Reece family were true, the meaning of those conversations would just be too horrifying.

"Come on, slowpoke," Marylis said turning to continue their walk at a little faster pace. "I'm dying to see your Granma's house."

"You saw it two days ago." Josh jogged to catch up with her.

"I fell in the door and got shoved right back out by your mom. I didn't see much."

"Granma can give you a tour later," Josh said with resignation. "Remember, we're going to see her to see what she knows, if anything, about that shadow-thingie."

Marylis sprinted ahead of him and knocked on Granma's door.

17

"So is there a map of this house?" Marylis asked Josh in a whisper as Granma led the two of them down the long central hallway toward the kitchen.

"Maybe, somewhere—" Josh started.

"Cool!" Marylis interrupted with a waver in her voice. She stopped by the fake doorframe. Tentatively she extended her fingers as if afraid the blank wall was hot. She ran her hand over the wallpaper pressing here and there like she was searching for some secret passageway.

"Marylis, it's just a wall and some molding. We're here about something important."

Granma stood peeking into the hallway through the kitchen window waiting for the two of them.

"Did that staircase in the entrance hall really go nowhere?"

"Marylis!" Josh said. He gave her a little shove toward the open window.

She stuck her tongue out at him.

He rolled his eyes.

"This is so neat," she felt the whole window frame before climbing through into the kitchen.

"I've made us a little snack," Granma said. She put a plate of barley and date cookies on the table next to a pitcher of milk. "One shouldn't learn frightening things on an empty stomach."

Josh rolled his eyes again.

Granma turned to get glasses for the milk.

Marylis reached for one of the cookies.

"Oh—" was all Josh could get out before she took a big bite.

She grimaced, chewed once more very slowly, and swallowed making a face that looked as if she were swallowing a live mouse. She smiled weakly at Granma as she took a glass of milk.

"How those cookies, Marylis?" Granma asked. "Josh loves 'em."

Marylis pooched out her cheeks as if they were full of cookie and nodded. She pretended to chew. Her eyes were still watering from that first bite.

While Granma's back was turned, Josh took a cookie, scraped at it with his fingernail over his plate until some crumbs fell off, and stuck the whole thing in his pocket.

Marylis followed suit and stuck the rest of her cookie in her pants pocket.

Granma rummaged around in the crisper at the bottom of the refrigerator. "Dang, I must have eaten the last of my celery," she muttered.

While Granma continued to search, Max hopped down to Marylis's plate. He eyed a large crumb for a second and then scooped it up with his beak. His little black eye seemed to widen and bug out a bit. He made a very small coughing sound and fluttered unsteadily back up to his customary perch.

Josh tried to keep the smile from his voice when he asked, "What now, Granma?"

She abandoned her celery search. "That sure was a quick snack!" She put the dishes in the sink and the rest of the cookies in the breadbox. "If those cookies are that good, I'm gonna have to see if I can sell that recipe!"

To the government's chemical warfare division maybe, Josh thought.

"Before we go upstairs…Marylis—"

Josh interrupted. He knew what Granma was going to ask. He'd seen her eyeing Max. "No, Granma, he won't poop on your rugs."

"I didn't think he would, Josh B'gosh. I was going to ask how she kept him from flying away because we're stepping outside once we get upstairs."

"Oh, he doesn't want to fly away. Max will be fine."

"Okay!" Granma did a John Wayne swagger and made the sign for 'wagons, ho!' and said, "Follow me, pahd'nas."

Josh's eyes were starting to hurt from all the rolling, but he rolled them again any way.

"Oh, boy!" Marylis said under her breath.

"Did you have any visions about this?" Josh asked in a whisper.

"I would have told you if I did, you dork," Marylis whispered back.

"I'm just waiting for one of your backwards visions to actually help us."

"Shut up," she hissed.

The three of them and Max left the kitchen and crossed the hall to climb the back stairs. Once on the second floor, Granma took two steps down the hall and stopped. In front of them was a doorframe that, like the one on the first floor, framed only wallpaper and paneling.

"Are we going up to Uncle Cecil's old room?" Josh asked.

"We are going to the attic," Granma said. She pushed on the wall. It creaked, resisting her push and then creaked on a different note as it slowly opened.

"Cool!" Marylis said again. "A fake door that's a real door."

"You don't have an attic, Granma," Josh said. He knew her house only had three floors. You could stand outside the house and see that. Even in this weird place you couldn't hide a whole floor of a house. Uncle Cecil's room was the only one on the third floor.

"Oh, I don't eh?" Granma said and she disappeared up the dark staircase casting spider webs to the floor as she cleared them away.

18

Josh wondered if his Uncle Cecil had had to climb up a dark staircase to bed each night. As far as Josh could remember, there had never been a light in here. "I really thought she'd take us to the library," he whispered. He felt bad about harassing Marylis about her visions. She obviously believed in them no matter how strange it seemed to him.

"She must have something here that's not even at the library," Marylis said with a tone between awe and reverence.

"But the only thing up here is Uncle Cecil's old room. I swear!"

At the third floor landing, Granma crossed the hall to his Uncle Cecil's room.

The two of them followed. Josh said, "I thought you told us we weren't going to Uncle Cecil's room?"

Granma turned. "Josh-B'gosh, sometimes you know more than you do." She patted him on the shoulder and smiled. "You ask questions before you observe all the facts in front of you and you judge too quickly. Have some patience. Sometimes, you should try not to be so much like your father."

She walked across the room and opened the window.

Josh felt a sudden, hot burst of anger in the center of his chest. What did she mean? Why had she said that? Just what was wrong with being like his father?

He opened his mouth to say something and realized he was alone in the room. Both of them had gone outside through the window. He rushed to follow and made it to the flat roof of the second floor just in time to see Marylis disappear around a corner.

When he caught up, Marylis whispered, "This is so neat."

Josh just grunted. Why was he so angry? He knew Granma had never really liked his dad. Was he mad just because she had mentioned him? Or was it because she'd said Josh was like his dad? And what did that mean anyway? Josh grunted again. Maybe he was just angry because she'd embarrassed him. He just knew Marylis would never let him forget this.

Granma yanked and grunted pulling at a weathered, wooden door.

"But that doesn't go anywhere," Josh said.

"Josh," Marylis whispered. "She lives here. I think she knows where she's going."

The door gave. It flew open hitting an interior wall with a bang. Without turning around, Granma caught it on the back swing before it hit her in the rear by lifting one foot. The door bounced off the flat of the sole of her shoe.

There was nothing but gray wall behind the open door.

Josh smiled an I-told-you-so smile at Marylis and pointed at the wall as if he were a host revealing a prize on a game show.

Granma lifted her other foot in the air and gave the wall in front of her two sound kicks. It swung open with a tooth-blistering squeak.

Marylis stuck her tongue out at Josh.

"THIS is the attic, Josh. Sorry about the smell. Somethin' must have died up here."

Josh sincerely hoped that that something wasn't a family member.

"Marylis, you might want to leave Max out here," Granma said, and she started spelling, "S-T-U-F-F-E-D P-A-R-R-O-T." She jerked her head twice in the direction of the open door.

"Can you cover it?" Marylis asked.

Granma winked and pointed an I-got-you finger at Marylis. She went into the room and two seconds later called, "Okay!"

Above their heads hung a single bulb in a cone of dented metal that looked as if it had been beaten against a wall, then painted green, then beaten against another wall. Next to it a skylight, imprinted with the skeletal outlines of leaves, let in a stained, brown light. Glass-fronted bookcases and metal, industrial shelving units lined the walls. There were wooden and wicker trunks in various stages of decay scattered about the baseboards. The side of one of the trunks had broken open, and silky clothes and bright feathery things had spilled out across the floor like colored water. There were stacks of magazines and a couple of old folding chairs. Ancient kerosene lanterns, ice skates that looked like deadly weapons, and old wreaths hung from the rafters and the walls.

An over-stuffed, cushy chair sat under a snake-necked reading lamp. Josh decided the chair must have either been built in the room or been here since the room itself was built. There was no way it could have fit through the door. Behind the chair and lamp was a suspiciously birdcage-y looking mound covered with a sheet.

"Where's the dressmaker's dummy?" Josh asked sarcastically. "It's the only thing missing."

Granma looked up from the stack of old newspapers she was flipping through. "Over by the moose head and the tuba."

And there it was. The moose head sat on the dress form's shoulders. It looked like some armless half-moose, half-woman monster. Josh closed his eyes and shook his head slowly.

"Josh-B'gosh, here's—"

"Granma please don't call me that," Josh said firmly.

She looked completely mystified. "Okay, Josh here's a picture of your Grandad's Uncle Percy," Granma said.

Josh and Marylis startled at the name of the man they had so recently been talking about. Both of them rushed over to her. It was a large, old photographic portrait of a dour looking man holding an open book up behind his head.

"It used to take so long to have a photograph made back then," Granma said. "Percy thought it was a waste of time. His wife Sissy made him sit for this one, and he insisted on being allowed to read while it was being taken."

Josh just stared at the picture. It made the back of his skull itch. He hoped he wasn't developing a third eye like his great granduncle was supposed to have had. The picture was a gag, Josh snorted. It HAD to be a gag.

"This isn't the one I was lookin' for, though." Granma went back to flipping through the portraits. "Here we go. Mason Reece, one of the founders of Rock Hollow."

This one was a painting. It looked familiar . . .probably from one of those boring old history books I poured over at the library yesterday, Josh thought.

"Hey! He looks like you!" Marylis said pointing at Josh and then back to the picture a couple of times in succession.

"Why, there is a family resemblance," Granma said nodding and tapping her lip with one finger.

"He looks like Percy," Josh said angrily. He could feel his face reddening. "I don't look anything like him."

Marylis and Granma giggled.

Josh started to ask why they were up here but Marylis piped up, "Mrs. Reece why is the house built like this? I mean all twisty with fake doors and stuff?"

"The short answer to that—all we have time for today—is that Macy Reece was terrified of spirits, and he built the dead-end hallways and stairways to nowhere to confound any dark thing that might not have his best interests in mind."

"Wow," Marylis stared down as if she could see the strange architecture through the floor.

Josh had never heard that particular tidbit of family lunacy. Now, he wished he hadn't. "Why were you looking for that picture?" He asked changing the subject and hoping it stayed changed.

Granma set the painting next to the chair. She pulled a crumbly looking leather bound book from one of the glass-fronted bookcases. "It's a visual aid, Josh-B'gosh. I'm gonna tell you a little of the story that's in this journal of his."

Josh just let that horrible, old nickname slide this time. "Why?" He asked.

Granma sat down in the big chair and turned on the light. "Because Mason's the one who got rid of the Shadowangel last time it came to town and stole the light from behind people's eyes." She opened the book carefully and flipped through hand-written pages of rusty words on yellowed paper. The whole thing looked as if it might crinkle to dust in a light breeze. "When old Colin Mikaplike seemed to have had a stroke, that was sad. In a town this size, when he was followed a couple nights later by Alan Prescot, that was passing strange. But Gertrude McGwinnon makes three, and that's a pattern. If you did see it attack Miss McGwinnon last night," Granma continued. "And, of course, I believe you did or we wouldn't be up here. You'll have to know how Mason Reece got rid of it; so's you can do it this time."

19

"I could really tell the story without the journal," Granma said. "But I know how you are, Josh. It's the closest thing I have to evidence that what I'm going to tell you is real."

Josh wanted to say something about how no amount of "evidence" would convince him some of her stories were true; but Marylis, who had just sat down, pulled on his pant-leg and pointed to a bare space on the dusty floor next to her. Even Max looked like he was ready for a story perched on the top of Marylis's head. For the first time since Josh met the bird, Max wasn't eyeballing him suspiciously. Max was facing forward and sitting (if birds sit) looking like nothing so much as an attentive preschooler waiting for story time to begin. Instead of protesting, Josh mentally shrugged and took a seat.

"This tale I'm going to tell you is the Readers' Digest Condensed version of the story. I've got twenty volumes of this man's journals," Granma continued. "And let me just say, he could bore the red out of a brick. To read his account of it, being a pioneer in the Northwest Territory was about as interesting as watchin' carrots grow."

Marylis giggled.

"Anyhoo, here we go: In 1791 Mason Reece and about twenty men set out from Marietta, Ohio to found a town halfway between there and Cincinnati. They were hoping this new town of theirs would become a way station for travelers between those two big cities. Well, they were big for the time. The men tromped all over these parts looking for the best place. They settled here, despite the fact that a lone Indian warned them against spending even one night in this Hollow."

"Does it say what the Indian said?" Marylis asked.

"American settlers weren't known for learning the native languages," Granma said. "So they had trouble understanding him. What they understood they called gibberish. Mason mentions two phrases: 'wings of night' and 'eater of light.' Like most white men of the period, they dismissed the Native American as a crazy savage and did what they wanted to. Everything went fine for a week or so. They had raised two cabins, so most of them weren't sleeping out under the stars any more. Just as they were planning the third cabin and contemplating sending to Marietta for some of the womenfolk, something strange

119

happened. Despite the fact that there was ample indoor space, some of the men were still sleeping outside. Mason and the others found one of those men just sorta sitting there staring. They couldn't rouse him. His eyes were dark, black really, almost to the edges like his pupils had dilated quite a bit beyond normal."

"So he'd had a stroke," Josh interrupted. He knew Miss McGwinnon hadn't had a stroke. And if Granma was telling them this story because of what they had seen, he knew that man, found in the same condition as Miss McGwinnon, hadn't had a stroke either. It just somehow felt better to pretend there was a rational explanation for everything.

"No, they didn't know what a stroke was back then. So they wouldn't have called it that, even if that was what it had been. It could maybe have been a stroke if it was an isolated incident. It wasn't. The next morning, another man was found the same way staring without sight, darkened eyes, unresponsive as a mannequin."

"Why didn't they all move inside?" Marylis asked.

"They did, the next night. They thought it was the Indians sneaking up and somehow poisoning the men. Those early people blamed every impediment and catastrophe they couldn't explain on the natives. Mason volunteered to keep watch. That next night after everyone had gone to sleep and both the sky and the cabins were dark, Mason saw it for the first time.

"A flitter of motion across a patch of open sky caught his attention. He thought he could make out something large and black. Thinking it was an unfamiliar species of bird, he watched as it flew around the two cabins. It landed just outside the door of one of them. He took his musket and his lantern over to investigate. The moment he saw it outlined against the cabin, he knew it was...wrong. He described it as 'darker than the night or the black of forest shadow.' He said he could only tell where it was 'from the absence of light in its vicinity.'

"What he saw next scared the starch outta his drawers. Before he could get to it, the thing got into the cabin. By the time he scrambled in after it, the thing had a man's arms in its grips," Granma flipped through some pages. She skimmed a page or two, seemed to find what she wanted and cleared her throat. She followed the text with her finger as she read. "'It appeared to consume a beam of light which it drew from behind his eyes. It was connected to him by this beam face-to-face, though this thing seemed to have no face at all.'"

Josh shuddered. He and Marylis looked at each other and they knew that this thing was what they had seen. They'd seen Miss McGwinnon in its claws, and they had seen the cone of light disappearing into its black, featureless face.

"So," Granma went on startling both her listeners. "Mason made a threatening noise, but it paid him no mind. He didn't think it a smart move to shoot at it since it was attached to the man it was attacking. He turned up the flame in his lamp. He wanted to club it with the butt of his musket, but he couldn't see well enough where to hit. As the circle of bright light from the lamp reached the thing, it screeched and let go of the man. Mason said right then the smell of charred meat filled the cabin.

"It turned to face Mason and sort of hung in the air flapping its huge wings. One of the others was awake enough to take a shot at it from the side. Mason saw the shot slam into it. He expected the monster to fall, but it kept hovering there, head bobbing slowly as if it was giving him the once over. Mason heard a thunk. The musket ball had fallen harmlessly out of the things belly. It had entered its side and exited its front without doing one whit of damage. The thing let out another screech and flew straight at Mason who was in the way of the door, you see. He got knocked on to his back and might have hit his head. But when he came to himself moments later, he described it as 'an angel clad in shadow.'"

20

"It didn't look anything like an angel to me," Josh said.

Marylis shook her head, "It looked more like a...a...an alien."

"Well, those early Americans probably hadn't even entertained the notion of life up there." Granma jabbed both thumbs at the ceiling. "Up there to them was Heaven, so it's not too strange they'd call it 'angel' if they thought that's where it came from."

"Why not demon?" Marylis asked. "Dark and scary and killing people sounds more like a demon than an angel."

Granma shrugged. "Well, remember not all angels turned out to be good in the end. Besides, given the length of his journals, Mason loved the sound of his own words, so he was probably trying to be flowery."

Josh cleared his throat and said, "So, how did they kill it?"

"Well, there were no locals that Mason and his men could talk to that they trusted. From their brief encounter, they figured they couldn't reason with this Shadowangel, find out what it wanted, or ask it to leave them alone. They decided to destroy it. People are always unnecessarily killing what they don't understand...this was one of those rare instances when that was pretty much the right answer."

"But HOW did they do it?" Josh prompted.

"Josh B'—Josh you would try the patience of Mahatma Gandhi! I am getting there."

He wanted to say "not fast enough." He wanted to ask why they didn't just go for help. He wanted to ask why they had to do anything about it themselves...but he kept his teeth clamped firmly on his tongue. He didn't want her angry like his mother had been, and he didn't want to hear again how much he was like his father.

"Their muskets hadn't fazed it, but they thought the light from Mason's lantern had hurt it some. That confused them since it had seemed to take in light from its victim's eyes. Then one of the men pointed out that the light it seemed to eat was a dim, feeble light. Perhaps a brighter light might hurt it. Mason and two other men went after it when morning came. They each had a lantern. When they found it in a nearby cave, they turned up their lanterns, but that only drove it further into the cave.

"Back at the cabins, Mason set to thinking. If the lamplight only drove it away, maybe concentrated light would kill it. Mason was sure he had the perfect tool. He always carried his collection of magnifying glasses with him. His favorite pastime was using them to write documents on very small things. Before he died, he had written the Declaration of Independence on a robin's egg and the Constitution on a sardine."

A quick glance at Marylis told Josh he was the only one who found that story outlandishly ridiculous, so he kept his mouth shut.

Granma continued "All the men stayed in one cabin that night. When the Shadowangel arrived at camp, they laid low until it entered the cabin. One of the men slammed and barred the door. Mason and another man turned up the lanterns and focused rays of light on the creature using Mason's magnifying lenses. According to Mason's journals, it was hard to keep the beams trained on it. It screeched and swooped around the cabin trying to get away. Its skin began smoking and it redoubled its efforts to escape dropping pieces of its flesh all around the cabin. It made a mess of the place, but in the end it fell to a pile of ashes."

Both Josh and Marylis stared at her, their mouths hanging open.

"That," Granma said. "Is how Mason got rid of the Shadowangel the first time it came to Rock Hollow."

Josh blinked and said, "And you expect us to attack that thing with lamps and magnifying glasses? Why don't we just go to the police now that we know what it is?"

"Josh," Marylis said. "Your mother didn't believe us twice."

"But Granma is with us now," Josh said. "She knows about it, and she's an adult."

"Josh, while I could probably get your mother to say she believed us, I wouldn't be any more successful at getting the police to help us than you would."

"Why not? Why wouldn't they listen to you?" Josh asked.

"Well, honestly Josh, most of the people in town aren't old Rock Hollow stock. Most around here are new comers, and they, like you, see the former town librarian as only slightly less loony than Miss McGwinnon."

Josh blushed again. "Granma—" he started.

She held up a hand. "Don't think I don't know what you think of the family and of me, Josh. Your mother thinks I'm eccentric, but you think I'm loopy as a hula-hoop factory." She waggled her hand to keep him from interrupting. "I have never told you an untruth about the

127

family. And soon as we get rid of the Shadowangel, you and I will take a tour of the records and photos in this attic. If you want to, that is."

There was silence in the room.

Josh stared hard at the floor. Granma was right about how he felt about her stories. He hated that she'd known all along. He felt guilty for disbelieving without even asking for proof. He was probably a really bad grandson for not just taking her at her word. He stared at the floor for a moment more.

"What do we do next?" He asked.

21

Granma sent Josh's mom home after dinner that evening. He didn't know how Granma had managed to convince his mom to let him stay, but she had. He also didn't know how Granma had convinced Marylis to leave Max at home. Marylis really was unnaturally attached to that parakeet.

As the clock approached the hour of seven, Josh and Marylis sat in silence fingering the apparatus they'd assembled while Granma went off in search of appropriate headgear. She said the right hats were essential to any successful venture.

On the kitchen table lay three high-powered flashlights with fresh batteries, three large magnifying lenses, and (at Josh's insistence) one large and sturdy baseball bat.

Josh's stomach growled. He hadn't eaten much for dinner. He still didn't feel like eating, but his stomach didn't seem to care about his feelings.

"I still want to know what it is," Marylis said.

"Unless it talks and Granma said it didn't way back when, we probably won't ever know. Of course we may not even survive," Josh said.

"Give me a break, Doomboy!" Marylis said flashing him a look of exasperated disbelief. "I mean: is it the inspiration of all the vampire stories throughout history? There weren't laboratories back in Mason's time, so it can't be an escaped experiment. Maybe it's some strange, rare creature that takes over two hundred years to hatch out of an egg laid by the creature Mason killed?" Her expression had changed to one full of wonder, wide eyes and a thoughtful smile.

Josh looked at her skeptically. "What? Do you work for the Weekly World News?"

She ignored him. "Or is it an alien come to look for its friend who never returned from that tiny blue planet, third from the sun?"

"You are seriously whacked," Josh said to Marylis. "I just want to get rid of it before it hurts anyone else."

There was another silence, which Marylis broke by asking in a very small voice, "Are you scared?"

He nodded. "But there will be three of us this time. We can protect each other."

Marylis smiled and nodded. "Why do we have to do it?" She asked. "Adults are such goobers. Why don't they believe what kids tell them?"

"You've got me. Maybe they're just too preoccupied with their own problems." A thought struck Josh. He smirked. "You know, it's always the kid who sees things first in the movies. Parents watch plenty of movies. You'd think they'd learn something and listen to us some of the time. Then again, things like this don't happen in the real world."

Marylis huffed in exasperation. "What are we standing in right now? The unreal world?"

"No, Rock Hollow is just...well, it just isn't normal."

Marylis rolled her eyes and shook her head. "To return to saner subjects: your Granma was right too. No one listens to older people either. My parents treat anyone over fifty like a certified nutburger, or they treat them like a baby."

Josh stared through the kitchen table and nodded. That was exactly the way his father was. Josh had heard his dad talk about older people at his office and their crazy ideas not fitting into the new century. Josh was certain he was nothing like his father in more ways than he WAS like him.

He had just opened his mouth to ask Marylis about her parents when Granma came barreling around the corner interrupting his train of thought. Josh took one look at what she carried, and he buried his face in his hands shaking his head.

"Here we are!" Granma said plopping a camouflaged-mosquito-netted army helmet on Marylis's head and holding up two identical helmets. "The perfect hats!"

22

They stood in front of the cold, black mouth of the tunnel. The green smell took Josh back to the moment before the Shadowangel burst out upon them last night. Had it really been only last night? It seemed like weeks ago; he wished it were months ago. He just kept hearing that umbrella sound and remembering the urge to reach up and touch it. He shivered thinking of Mason's description of the musket ball just dropping out of its body. "I don't know about this," he said.

"Oh, come on!" Marylis said. "We have to check it out. This is where we found it last night."

"But maybe we scared it out of here," Josh said. "It wasn't under the Nicholson's eaves, and we found it there night before last."

"Come on, Josh-B'gosh." Granma said.

"Granma! That's a baby nickname. Please don't call me that!"

"Okay. Okay. Just give me some time. You still are a baby to me."

He opened his mouth to protest, but her wink silenced him. "Come on. I'll go first." She turned on her flashlight, bent over slightly, and tromped into the darkness.

Marylis followed.

Josh didn't want to follow.

He sighed. He checked for the baseball bat that he'd strapped to his back with an old belt. He snapped on his flashlight and entered the darkness.

The water and algae made the floor slippery, so they walked as much as possible on the concrete just above the water line. The beams of their flashlights looked like yellow-white light sabers spinning wildly around the walls of the tunnel up ahead. Once they were deep in the throat of the tunnel, the trickle of the water became magnified to the hissing roar of river rapids.

"THERE'S—" Marylis started to speak in her normal voice. The echo made it so loud that she switched to a whisper to be understood. "—There's no place it could sit or—well, hang even—without getting wet."

"Maybe it doesn't mind that," Granma said.

This whole monster hunt was a stupid idea, Josh thought. They knew the thing was dangerous. Sure, they knew how some old pioneer guy had killed something like it once. Josh knew how pioneer guys killed bears; that did not mean he was planning on going on a bear hunt any time soon. They just didn't know enough about this thing yet. But then, where were they likely to learn more than they had in Mason's journal?

Josh kept looking over his shoulder. Behind them, the evening light from the mouth of the tunnel had vanished completely. There was only the dark. Josh was certain they couldn't have missed the monster lurking in the part of the tunnel they had checked already, but the empty blackness behind him made his back feel vulnerable every time he faced forward. At least the darkness in front of them was broken by the sweep of their flashlight beams.

The roar of the water drowned out the normal night sounds from the world above. Between that and the darkness, he felt completely cut off from everyone and everything else.

"Look!" Marylis whispered loudly.

Josh nearly jumped out of his shoes.

He smacked her on the back, but followed the beam of her light. Halfway up the wall, a smaller pipe broke through the wall of the main pipe. Though it was dry now, it had obviously spit water into the creek at one time because brittle, brown dried up algae hung down from its lower lip.

"There must be more of these," Marylis whispered. "We heard water from one when we were here before. It's definitely big enough for the Shadowangel to scrunch into."

Granma said, "Yes."

"Well, let's watch out for them then," Josh said and he nudged both of them into moving again. *The sooner we get out,* Josh thought, *the sooner we get out!*

They passed two of those smaller pipes that trickled with water, or something that had the same liquid properties as water. Who knew where it came from? Street run-off, factory waste…town toilets. In the light from their flashlights, it looked a little too chunky for Josh to feel comfortable calling it water. Still, no light from the far end of the tunnel reached them. Josh kept his light angled out in front of them aimed at about the height of the tributary tunnels they'd seen. The dark seemed to settle against his skin like a second shirt. It almost seemed to press in on him. Despite the coolness of the air, the stench of the algae made it hard to breathe without gagging.

"Have you noticed—" Josh started.

An ear-drilling screech filled the tunnel with sound and startled them all in to silence.

23

Marylis screamed.

Granma pulled out her magnifying glass. She focused the beam to a pinprick on the tunnel wall in front of them.

Marylis clamped her mouth shut. Her magnified scream reverberated and echoed back diminishing slowly as she followed Granma's lead.

Josh was in a quandary; he fingered his flashlight with one hand and reached for the handle of his baseball bat with the other. The certainty and the physicality of a good hard whack with the bat seemed a much surer thing than a weak beam of insubstantial light. He wrestled the baseball bat free of its harness and clutched it before him samurai-style with both hands. "Please tell me in one of your reverse psycho visions you saw us all get horribly slaughtered," Josh whispered urgently to Marylis's back.

She turned around and slapped him in the stomach with the flat of her magnifying glass. "It's coming, you freak, be serious!"

I was, he thought, holding the bat ready to thwonk whatever came out of the tunnel.

The screeching rose in pitch and volume. It obviously came from the tributary tunnel a few feet in front of them, and it was definitely getting closer.

He didn't want to drop his bat, but Josh desperately wanted to cover his ears. He was beginning to feel the screech deep inside his ear canal.

Something jerked into view in the darkness. It slammed first into one side of the pipe and then the other. The dark mass barreled toward them through the shadows. As it entered the area of weak light in front of the monster hunters, the three could tell it was far too small to be the Shadowangel. The screeching continued less echoey and ominous now that it was in the main part of the tunnel, and two large rats tumbled into the light rolling over and over each other. Chunks of their fur flew into the air like feathers from a pillow fight.

They leapt off of each other and hissed at Granma and Marylis's lights. Their red-black eyes flashed like blood rubies in the high-powered beams. They stood up on their haunches and offered one last yellow-toothed hiss before running off down the main tunnel.

Josh, Marylis, and Granma finally exhaled a breath none of them knew they'd been holding.

Granma turned. The light from her flashlight stretched her features making her face look like a poorly cast rubber mask. "What was that about visions and slaughter?"

Josh didn't trust himself to explain. He was afraid his skepticism would color what he said. Hoping she wouldn't guess why, he motioned for Marylis to go ahead.

Marylis cast her eyes downward. She scraped at a patch of dried algae with the toe of one of her sneakers.

Josh couldn't believe she was holding back. She and Granma seemed to get along so well. They seemed more related than he and Granma did. He placed his fingers gently on her shoulder and nudged her.

"I—uh I—" She just stopped.

For Pete's sake, Josh thought. Placing all of the conviction he could into his voice, he said, "She's reverse psychic, Granma. She has visions of the future; but if she sees something happening, it definitely won't. In fact, if she sees something in a vision, the opposite usually happens."

Marylis turned such a grateful smile on Josh that he felt his cheeks redden. *Please let it be too dark in here for them to see me blushing*, he thought. *Granma would tease me for weeks.*

"That so, Marylis?" Granma asked without a trace of disbelief in her voice.

"Yes. Josh is really the only one I've ever told about it except my Granny."

Josh felt his blush deepen. He cleared his throat and peered ahead of them into the darkness. Trying to change the subject, he said, "Hey, I can see the light of the tunnel exit up ahead."

"I don't think it's in here," Marylis said.

He couldn't believe how disappointed she sounded. He was relieved.

"Well, Marylis, have you seen anything that would help us?" Granma asked.

"Not that I can make any sense of," she answered.

"You two have seen it before. Where to next?" Granma asked.

For a moment no one said anything.

"Well, how about we check out Miss McGwinnon's?" Josh asked. "There's no one living there. She's at the hospital. Maybe it slept there. It could even have slept inside the house." Remembering how cluttered her living room had looked, Josh bet there were plenty of dark and dingy crevices the thing could use to wait out the day.

Granma and Marylis nodded grimly. They looked nearly as thrilled as Josh felt about the prospect of entering Miss McGwinnon's house. The three of them tromped around the last bend in the tunnel.

When they exited the concrete pipe, the sky was darker than Josh had expected. Against the pitch dark of the tunnel the waning light of evening had seemed bright. Now that they were out, he was surprised he'd noticed what light there was beyond the tunnel's opening. Josh re-holstered his baseball bat behind his back.

As they climbed up the embankment to Marble Street, he opened his mouth to ask what time it was when Marylis interrupted him with a loud whisper.

"We can't let anyone at my house see me," She glanced side-wise across the street at her house.

"And, why's that?" Granma said eyeing her suspiciously.

Marylis hesitated. "I'm kinda breaking curfew, and I'm a little grounded because of last night."

"A little grounded?" Granma said skeptically.

Josh rolled his eyes. His Granma was never going to say, "Marylis your parents punished you for a good reason. Now go on home." She wouldn't even say that if they were just out goofing around. Despite their similarities, Marylis had a lot to learn about Granma.

"Well it's for a good cause," Granma said with a wink. "If we move fast and stay low, they won't see us."

The three of them jogged around the corner and jumped into the woods at first opportunity. In his mind's eye, Josh could just see the three of them, camouflage helmets, flashlight-weapons, dark clothes. They probably looked like three short, clumsy, confused commandos.

"We should check the summer house too," Marylis said.

They advanced slowly through the trees toward Miss McGwinnon's. The house rose up against the sky like a substantial shadow of a much larger building. Josh felt two inches high. He could sense the emptiness of the house from across the yard. It seemed twice as spooky as the night before. Every window was an eye. . .or a convenient place for something to hide before ambushing an unsuspecting trio of inexperienced monster hunters.

They came free of the trees. Josh looked tentatively up at the sky. He knew he was being silly, but he could feel it out there in the night.

Without warning, a large hand clamped over Josh's mouth, and an arm wrapped around his waist. He kicked his feet, reached for the handle of his bat, tried to struggle free, but he was pulled away from Granma and Marylis and back into the woods.

24

"You won't get away this time, Cracker," Hannibal whispered in Josh's ear as he dragged him back toward the street. "I'm going to beat you to a pulp before you can yell for help."

Josh tried again to pull free. He wondered if Han had worked all day on that little rhyme. Struggling and twisting to get away, he caught a glimpse of Han's face and was sure the bully hadn't even noticed he's said something funny. Han's hair stuck out in every direction. His dark button eyes glittered with malice. His apish, overhanging upper lip was drawn back in a sneer.

"Nah Ahh! Nobody makes me look stupid and walks away without somethin' broken on em'."

Your personal medical bill must be astronomical, Josh thought. *Just think how many times you've made yourself look like an idiot in the couple days I've known you.*

"Now you're hanging out with my retard sister," Han said squeezing Josh so tightly he thought he felt his eyes bug out. "Once we're done with you, she'll get hers."

Josh knew he had to think fast. "We" might mean the goons couldn't be far off even if he couldn't see them at the present moment. He knew he couldn't get to the baseball bat harnessed to his back or the flashlight in his belt with his arms pinned. Fortunately, Granma and Marylis would come looking for him in a minute or two. Unfortunately, Han and company could probably do quite a bit of damage in even that short of a time.

Josh bit down hard on the fleshy part of Han's palm. He tasted blood.

Han yelped and let go of Josh's mouth shaking his wounded hand in the air.

Josh didn't waste time yelling for help. That would be expected. He elbowed Han in the gut as hard as he could. At the same time, he rocked forward onto the balls of his feet and brought both of his heels down on the instep of one of Han's feet.

Han let go of Josh's waist.

Josh spun around pushing away from his attacker.

Han, bent double, staggered back a step. He tried unsuccessfully to catch his breath sounding like he was having the granddaddy of all hiccough fits.

Josh placed one hand in the middle of Han's head and shoved.

The bully toppled over. The thud of his weight and the crack of sticks and twigs beneath him were accompanied by a sound like a child's squeaky toy as the very last bit of air left his lungs. For a minute, his feet worked the air as if they thought he was taking a Sunday stroll. He reminded Josh of a giant Galapagos tortoise caught on its shell in the sun.

Josh heard a thrashing in the woods in the direction of the road. He looked up. In the darkness, he could just make out two whitish circles bobbing back and forth above the underbrush. Goon #1 and Goon #2 were headed right for him.

He turned again and ran for Granma and Marylis.

25

Josh ran out into Miss McGwinnon's yard. He'd successfully extracted the baseball bat from its harness. He carried it and the flashlight like clubs, one in each hand.

Granma and Marylis were just turning around to look for him.

"Where'd you go?" Marylis asked, her hands on her hips.

He had to breathe between each word, but he said, "Your jerkwad brother followed us."

Marylis stomped her foot. "Crud!" She said.

"He's got his goons with him now," Josh said.

Marylis said something that, in the presence of any parent, would have won her a trip to her room...or a date with a Dial soap lollipop.

Granma, unfazed by Marylis's language, patted the girl on her back. "Now, don't worry. We have bigger bunnies to burn. They won't come near you two while I'm here."

Marylis didn't look convinced. Despite the fact that Granma's presence had made Hannibal turn tail once, Josh was thinking things might be different in front of his henchdorks. He was just about to say as much when he saw a streak of black slide across the darkening sky. He pointed to it with the bat. He'd never been fond of war movies, but for some strange reason he felt like shouting, "Incoming!" When he did shout, both Marylis and Granma turned and stared at him with expressions of disbelief and amusement.

"Come on, you all! Let's follow it!" Granma yelled. They set off walking swiftly across Miss McGwinnon's yard.

"It's headed toward the park," Marylis said.

"And most of the rest of the houses in town," Granma added.

For a moment, Josh was relieved that his mom was safely in their house behind them to the southeast. Then his misbehaving mind offered up a horrifying thought. Southeast was the direction from which it seemed to be flying. There wasn't a lot out there, the highway to Cincinnati, a bunch of trees, and a couple of houses. "Ma-maybe it's already. . .fed," he said.

"It seems too early in the night—" Marylis stopped herself mid-sentence.

Even in the dark Josh could tell from her expression something was wrong.

"What is it, Marylissie?" Granma said.

"My house!" Marylis gasped. "In that direction, it's the first house that thing will reach!" She launched herself into the woods.

Josh set off at a run after her. Granma took up the rear.

"Turn on your flashlight, Josh!" Granma yelled from behind him.

He turned his on without slowing down. "Marylis," he yelled. "Turn on your light!"

After a moment, a bobbing beam appeared between the trees in front of him.

He caught up with her just as she stepped out onto Marble Street. The Shadowangel glided over her house. Stars winked as it passed. It cut back and circled just as it had the night before at Miss McGwinnon's. Josh shuddered as he watched it. When it moved he thought of those stop-action animated characters in old monster movies. Just like them it moved with an awkward jerkiness. It looked pasted on to the world around it. The Shadowangel landed soundlessly on the branch of a tree directly across the street from Marylis's house. For one crazy moment, its tiny head lolling at the end of its long neck reminded Josh of Snoopy's vulture impersonation from *Peanuts* cartoons.

"I know you don't really want any of them to get hurt," Josh said. "But at the very least I expected a snide comment about how anyone in your family would give it indigestion before you took off to help them."

"You don't understand," She said never taking her eyes off the creature in the tree. "Mom and Dad are in Cincinnati tonight. If Han's in the woods behind us—"

"The house is empty," Josh offered with a hopeful shrug.

"No," Marylis said. "My Granny Addie's in there, and she can't even get out of her bed by herself."

26

Granma came out of the woods behind them. She must have heard what Marylis said. "It's been so long since I heard from your Granny Addie, Marylis." She laid her free hand gently on Marylis's shoulder. "I was sure they'd packed her off to some home."

"It's cheaper to keep her here and keep her Social Security check," Marylis said in a sour voice.

Josh thanked his lucky stars for his wonderful mother and Granma who despite their differences really seemed to like each other most of the time. "So what do we do?" He asked. "Do you think we should whisper? Can it understand us? Does it even have ears?"

"Let's zap it, now!" Marylis said loudly.

Josh cringed at her volume. The Shadowangel was only about forty or fifty feet away across Silver street. It didn't move or startle or give any indication that it had heard or sensed them in any other...or otherworldly way. Still, when he spoke, Josh whispered hoping she would do the same, "I know that's the idea; I meant how do we go about it?"

"We can't let it get near the house!" Marylis insisted.

Josh shushed her. "We weren't planning to. But if we attack it out here, it could just fly away."

"You don't understand," she said in a voice a hair's breadth from a shout. "I think I DID have a vision last night."

"'You think'?" Granma asked.

"My visions are a lot like dreams. I just thought it was too silly to mention. It was of my granny...she killed the Shadowangel with her reading lamp while Josh and I hid our eyes."

"If our eyes were closed, how did you see your Granny kill it?" Josh asked.

Marylis rounded on him. "It was a dream. I was watching everything from the outside!"

He held up his hands. "Okay, okay...I don't have a lot of experience with these kinds of things."

Granma leaned in close to whisper, "Marylis, you said they needed interpreting. How would you interpret that vision?"

Trying to be helpful, Josh started, "That could mean...I don't know."

"It means," Marylis said with urgency. "That it will kill Granny Addie while we watch!"

"We just won't let it near the house," Granma said quietly, calming her with a pat on the back. "Let's surround it before we shine our lights on it. That might work."

Josh and Marylis nodded and turned off their flashlights.

Marylis circled around behind it. After a few steps she disappeared into the night fog that had risen from the creek and the pond while they'd been in the woods. It was as if she plunged face first into a charcoal colored pool. The fog closed behind her like liquid night.

Granma approached it from where they'd stood.

Josh put himself between the Shadowangel and Marylis's house. He couldn't see Granma or Marylis. That, in itself, was unsettling. What if it had brought a friend tonight? Its buddy could swoop down on any of the three of them and the other two would never know. *Shut up shut up*, he told his misbehaving mind. The fog felt like the cold, damp caresses of unseen hands. It conspired with the dark to hide everything but the tree and the Shadowangel.

"On three," Granma said in a hoarse whisper just loud enough for him to hear. "One--Two--THREE!"

Josh flicked on his light and focused the beam at the creature.

A second beam came from the same direction as Granma's voice.

The thing in the tree screeched. There was enough light for Josh to see smoke rise from the beast. Two tiny bright spots winked into being and glowed like ember eyes, one on its shoulder and another in the center of its chest.

Marylis's light didn't appear.

HAN! Josh thought. *It had to be Han and his goons. Now what do we do?*

The Shadowangel jumped from the branch and headed, not toward the house, but toward Marylis.

A high-pitched scream rang out in the darkness.

27

When Josh got to Marylis, she was beating at the Shadowangel with the bulb end of her flashlight.

It had latched on to a wildly screaming Han. Its grip on his upper arms kept him from hitting it, but he was shaking himself back and forth and running around while flapping his forearms uselessly. Marylis did her best to keep up getting a good whack when she got close enough.

Granma arrived just behind Josh. As one, they swung the beams of their lights in the direction of the beast focusing on its dark skin as best they could.

The thing screeched and let go of Han. It launched itself into the air blowing the dusty smell of ashes and the copper-in-your-mouth scent of blood into their faces with each wing beat.

Han just kept screaming rolling around in the leaves and dirt as if his clothes were on fire. His eyes stayed closed. He batted and swatted at nothing with his flailing hands.

"His Goons ran off into the woods when they saw it," Marylis said catching her breath.

Josh nodded. He had the feeling that if they got through this, those bullies wouldn't be much trouble to him or Marylis anymore. *If we get through this*, Josh thought, *we will have dealt with much worse.*

Josh started to bend over Han who was still squealing like some cartoon parody of a lady who has seen a mouse.

"Leave him," Granma said. "He may be damp and dusty and scared, but he's all right."

Marylis grabbed Josh's sleeve and pulled him back toward her house. Over her shoulder she said, "Come on! It's going to get inside!"

The house came into view through the mist just in time for them to see the thing land on the porch railing.

They dashed across the street.

The Shadowangel hopped down and wobbled sickly toward the front door.

They crossed the yard.

It butted its head through the screen of the door, ripped at the nylon material with its claws, and pulled itself through the jagged opening.

By the time they got to the end of the front walk, the Shadowangel was already out of view somewhere in the dark house.

28

As Josh ran up the steps to the front door he said, "Where is your Granny?"

Marylis jumped ahead of him and jerked open the door. "Come on!" she yelled.

The house looked as if it had never seen a proper cleaning. *If it were less messy,* Josh thought, *I might ask if there'd been some kind of explosion. I've seen better housekeeping on "Hoarders."*

Marylis took the stairs two at a time.

Josh followed suit.

The two of them rounded a corner in the upstairs hallway.

The shadowangel was moving as if it were wounded, so he and Granma must have had some effect on it. As they neared it, he could see a gray patch on its shoulder that seemed to grow bigger as he watched. He bet there was one on its chest as well. It dragged itself toward an open door at the far end of the hall. Through the doorway, the soft light of a TV flickered creating patterns like spirits on the walls. "Marylis?" came a voice from the room.

"Close your eyes, Granny Addie!" Marylis yelled. "Close 'em quick, I've got a surprise for you!"

Josh and Marylis were right behind the thing as they entered the room. Both turned their flashlight beams on it and stepped out of the way of the door. They needed to get it out of the room before it got a hold of Marylis's granny. Marylis sidled around it to the right to stand between her Granny Addie and the thing. Josh inched to the left to get between it and the open but screened window. They focused their beams on the Shadowangel.

It screeched like a wildcat in pain and wheeled around to make for the door. Josh really didn't care if it got away at this point. He didn't care, just as long as everyone here was safe...even Han.

Granma appeared in the doorway and focused her beam on the thing too.

Its screech rose in pitch. It began to smoke and shake like a pressure cooker with a full head of steam.

It swung toward Josh as if it were trying to bite him with a non-existent mouth. Its head whipped around and lashed out at Marylis.

The thing's squeal just kept getting louder. Josh gritted his teeth against the pain in his ears.

Finally, the shadowangel's legs gave. It hit the ground. The impact made it pop like a soap bubble: an enormous soap bubble full of ashes. A fountain of gray flakes geysered toward the ceiling, and a gray snow floated around the room and fell to coat the walls, the furniture, and the floor.

Marylis kicked at the ashes furiously until all around her, they were ground into the carpet or scattered elsewhere across the bedroom floor.

29

"Marylis? What was all that racket? Should I open my eyes now? Did you bring me a present?" Marylis's granny opened her eyes and looked from one of them to another. "Hi Risa!" she said to Josh's Granma.

Granma huffed out a breath and waved.

Marylis just stared at her soot stained shoes and the huge greasy, gray stains on the carpet.

The quiet got to Josh first. "Uh, Hi! I'm Josh, Marylis's friend. We—uh—we were bringing my Granma over to say hey to you—and we—um we saw this huge rat. We chased it around the house. And—uh Marylis didn't want you to be scared, so she told you to close your eyes." He smiled and made a weak attempt at laughing.

Marylis's Granny raised one eyebrow. "Hmm. Don't think I've ever seen a giant rat with wings...and I know I've never seen a rat turn to ashes when you shine a flashlight on it neither."

"Granny," Marylis said finally looking up. A smile spread across her face, "You peeked."

Granny Addie smiled too. "When all you got to entertain you is the idiot-box," she gestured to a small old-fashioned square television now covered with ashes that sat at the end of her bed. "You're not about to pass up the chance to see somethin' someone doesn't want you to. 'Sbeen my experience them are the best things to see, so when you hollered at me to close my eyes...well...that was like an invitation."

Granma giggled. Marylis's smiled broke into laughter. Josh rolled his eyes and shook his head. But, in a moment, he was laughing too.

"So what was it, Risa?" Marylis's Granny asked. "And how did you come to be standing here in my bedroom covered with ashes, leaves, and sticks?" She paused and looked around the room. "Guess I know where the ashes came from. You look like some crazed mountain woman, and you smell like granddad's outhouse after the goat fell in. Come, sit here and tell me the whole story." She patted the bed next to herself.

"Well," Granma said. "It all started this time (and I'll get to the first time in a minute) when my Grandson there come back to town with his mother—"

"Oh, isn't that nice! Lisa's back in town!" said Marylis's granny.

"Yep. Anyhoo, the other day…"

Marylis and Josh weren't about to listen to Granma's take on the whole story. They crept out into the hall and sat down, leaning against the wall and each other.

"I should call my mom," Josh said. "Granma told her something to get rid of her tonight. I don't know what it was. Knowing Granma and her storytelling, I think I better find out."

"Let's rest for a minute," Marylis said with a sigh. "Do you really think it's gone?"

"I really think it's all over your shoes," Josh answered.

Marylis half-smiled and gently punched his shoulder.

"What about that vision of yours?" he asked.

"I told you they needed interpreting." She seemed to think for a minute. "I guess the reverse of my vision wasn't it killing her instead of her killing it. The reverse was us killing it while her eyes were closed instead of her killing it while our eyes were closed."

"Oh, okay," Josh said. *I don't understand*, he thought. *I will never understand, so I will just smile.*

"NOW what are we going to do for excitement?" She asked.

Josh smacked her on the shoulder. "We're going to go to school and do our homework and watch too much television and talk about videogames and try to be as normal as possible. That's what."

Marylis hit him back, "You are so weird! There IS no such thing as NORMAL. Everyone everywhere from Portland Maine to Portland Oregon, for now and always, since the cavemen and until the sun dies, was…is and will be W-E-I-R-D! Normal is a myth!"

Josh just shook his head.

Marylis stood up and dragged him to his feet. "Let's go check on Max," she said. "Then you can call your mom." They set off down the hall toward her room.

Wrongeye, Or--A third resident of the small
Mountain town of Wrongeye was
found in a catatonic state this morning.
Doctors have been unable to draw
any response from either of the other
two discovered on Monday and
Tuesday respectively. Each of the
victims of this strange affliction
lived alone or were alone for a time
before they were discovered. This latest
victim was Mrs. Gladys Hondola.
Authorities fear this may be an epidemic
of an as yet undiscovered disease. Some of
the more colorful residents seem to think
this is the work of "a winged black
monster." Mrs. Hondola will join
the others...

About the Author:

Tim Capehart is the author of "Seeking the Link," a collection of short stories for adults and young adults. Many of those stories appeared in magazines and newspapers before he collected them himself in 2008 (Still available in paperback on Amazon.com!). He has been writing since the second grade when he hid in a corner with a typewriter and banged out a tale of a horse that ate hotdogs (a tale based in fact). He has a Creative Writing degree from Miami University and a Masters of Library Science from University of Kentucky. He is a Children's Librarian and has been on the Newbery Committee twice (so far). He has written book reviews for nearly every magazine in Library-land that publishes them. Currently, he writes several reviews for each issue of the bi-weekly Kirkus Reviews. He also blogs frequently at timothycapehart.weebly.com when not working on a book. He lives in Dayton, Ohio with his partner Trent and two pretty fabulous felines who also write book reviews on his blog; cats have opinions too!

Acknowledgements:

I always have to acknowledge Trent for putting up with me especially when I am working on a book...which is nearly always even if it's only in my head. This time I would also like to thank my early readers: Dad and Mom (of course) and Pam, Rob, Abby and Zach Schultz. All of them provided suggestions and guidance. I would also like to thank Ginny Rorby for pointers and confidence and Jennifer Holm for trying REAL hard. I thank and love you all. And finally, one must always acknowledge one's cats; you never know what they'll do if you don't. So, thank you Banjo and Bubble and your spirit sisters Bruegel and Buffy Sainte Meow. Over the years, all of them put up with me staring at the glowey box instead of playing Mousie or Fishie or Pink Baby...thankfully Lap appears when a human stares at the glowey box; that's some consolation.

CPSIA information can be obtained at www.ICGtesting.com
Printed in the USA
LVOW05s2304210114

370455LV00011B/302/P

9 781484 920169